Mists of
Bayou Rhyne

❧❧❧❧❧❧

ISBN: 978-0-9961483-0-6

Cover design: Black Calla Press
Cover illustration: Michael Jarusiewicz

Printed in the United States of America

❧❧❧❧❧❧

To Becky, my beautiful daughter, and to Alyssa and Seth for
giving life a purpose.

I love you.

CHAPTER ONE

"Belle, will you watch out? You drive like a freakin' *drunk*." Jess Winslow said as they pulled the little black Mercedes C350 coupe up to Lloyd Aubrey's. The music blared through the open windows and kids laughed and roamed the premises inside and out, each with some sort of drink in hand.

As Belinda Larson and Jess made their way up the steps, a girl sitting on the white railing of the porch slapped the boy leaning into her. "Get off me, you moron!"

Jess snickered. "Seems like everyone's already plastered and it's only nine o'clock."

Some guy rushed down the stairs and plowed into Belinda, catching her arm before she tumbled back. "Whoa, sorry." He glanced at her with recognition. "Hey, Belinda. Glad you made it."

"Yeah, thanks." Belinda pushed away from him, pulling her tight black skirt down and straightening her equally tight low-cut top. "Hey, do you know if Derrick Anderson is here yet?"

"Derrick? I heard he wasn't coming," the boy said as he continued down the steps. "Hey, go inside and have some fun. They're doing keggers in the kitchen," he said and ran toward the over-sized water fountain where several kids were splashing each other.

The large house was crammed with kids, some dancing in the living room, others lining the stairwell, and still others taking up every inch of the halls — it was as if the whole school had shown up.

"Man, this place is packed," Belinda yelled over the music. She pointed toward the back down the long hallway. "That must be where the kitchen is. Come on."

They pushed through the swinging doors and found several kids lying across the island in the center of the kitchen, their heads hanging off the edge. Another kid leaned over them holding a tube that extended from the keg letting the flow of beer rush into their open mouths. One boy bolted upright after the first mouthful, coughing, and hit his head against the pots and pans hanging above the table. He reached up to stop them from clanging and sent several crashing to the floor.

"I'm next," yelled Belinda.

Jess tugged on her arm. "You sure that's a good idea?"

"Lighten up, Jess, you're starting to annoy me," Belinda said and pulled away. "Besides, you're the DD tonight."

"Since when am I the designated driver? You hate the way I drive."

"Since I want to get drunk and you're all I have." Belinda walked over to the table and leaned over the girl on the table. "Get up. I said I'm next."

The girl rolled her eyes, but moved off the table as she was told.

Belinda lay in her place, laughing. "Don't get that crap on my clothes, moron," she warned the boy with the keg, "or you're dead."

"Yeah, no problem," he said. "Head back."

The room spun when Belinda sat up. She giggled and slid off the table. Jess had to reach to steady her.

"Jeez, Belle. Get a grip," Jess said.

Belinda giggled some more. "I'm fine. It just hit me funny when I got up so quickly. I'm fine now." She ran her fingers through her hair, and turned to the guy with the keg. "Hey, jackass, you got it in my hair."

"Go in the pool and wash it out," someone shouted.

"I didn't bring a bathing suit."

The boy with the keg grinned. "You wearing a bra and panties under that sexy outfit?"

"Panties," she said with a smirk.

"Then you have a bathing suit. Nothing more needed," the boy said. "Besides, before the nights out we'll all be skinny dipping, anyway."

Belinda laughed and tugged on Jess's arm, pulling her down the hall. "Come on, let's check it out."

Half-naked teens crowded the pool. Belinda and Jess sat at the edge of the pool and dangled their feet in the water.

Belinda's mood swung low. "Hey, Jess, you think Derrick will stop by?"

Jess rolled her eyes. "If he isn't here by now, chances are he won't be. Give it a rest, will you?"

"I want to see him," Belinda mumbled more to herself than to Jess.

"Didn't he say he was watching the Rhyne property while they were out of town?" Jess asked.

"You're right! Come on, Jess. Let's blow this place. I think I want to stop by the barn to check on Goliath," Belinda said with a devilish giggle.

"I'd rather not," Jess said. "Besides, what's the big deal with Derrick anyway? He's with Cassie and blows you off constantly. You might think you'd get the hint. He.Ain't.Interested."

"Yeah, that's what you think. He's more interested than you know. Didn't you see the way he smiled at me at the 7-11 store the other night?"

"God, Belle, he smiles at everyone. He was just being nice."

Belle tsked. "What's your problem? Don't you think I'm pretty enough to get Derrick?"

"It's not about being pretty. He's with Cassie. He's taken. You know, off the market. So why do you bother when you can pretty much have anyone else you want?"

"Because I want Derrick, that's why. Cassie doesn't deserve a guy like him. He's way too good for her. I want him, and I will have him."

"You're wicked."

Belinda smirked. "Maybe I am."

###

The old plantation house at the end of the long dirt road loomed before them. Small statues of jockeys stood beneath the tall moss dripped oak trees, grotesquely masked in the late night shadows, their dimly lit lanterns lighting the way.

"This place looks scary at night," Jess said. "Of course it doesn't help that it's about to rain any second. It couldn't be any darker. Or creepier." She shuddered. "Do we have to go? Don't you want to go back to the party?"

"Oh, shut up," Belinda said and took a swig from the Captain Morgan she'd stolen on their way out of the party. She peered out the windshield. The large tree trunks spread their spidery branches and cast the ominous illusion of witches' fingers reaching toward their car. She winced. "Actually, you're right. Scary."

Jess continued to the blue barn, located to the right of the house, at a crawl. Belinda stumbled out of the car as soon as it was parked, laughing into the palm of her hand, and leaned on the car door for support.

"Man, you're drunk," Jess said.

"No, I'm not. Just a little…tipsy."

"Leave the bottle in the car."

"Shh, where do you think Derrick is?" Belinda asked and took another sip of the rum.

Jess left the headlights on and moved around the front of the Mercedes. "My guess would be the guest house near the lower barn."

"You're probably right. Now where is that exactly?" Belle giggled.

"You've been here a dozen times. If you weren't so drunk, you'd know." Jess noticed a dim light coming from the window of the small ranch house near the red barn. "There. There's a light on inside."

Belinda wandered toward the sliding door of the big blue barn and shoved it open. Some of the horses snickered and pawed at their doors. She stumbled inside and staggered from one stall to the next, talking to each horse, until she reached Goliath's stall. "Here's my baby. How's my big boy?" She reached into the bag hanging on the front of the door and pulled out some pressed apple and oat snacks. She fed him one through the metal bars, cooing to him under her breath. She glanced out of the barn at Jess, still standing in the headlights of the car. "You coming in, or what?"

"What are we doing here? I don't like it, Belle," Jess said and walked toward her. "We shouldn't be here."

"Stop whining and flip that switch to your right."

Jess did as she was told and the center set of lights lit up overhead.

Belinda took another swig from the bottle and wiped her mouth with the back of her hand. "I'm saying hello to my horse. I have every right to be here." She scratched Goliath's nose through the metal bars. "Hi, sweetie," she murmured. "Did you miss me?"

Belinda grabbed Jess's arm as she neared. "You hear that? Sounds like a—"

"What are you two doing here?" Derrick Anderson said. He stepped in the doorway and glared at Belle. "Well?"

Belinda lost her balance as she spun around and had to grab onto Goliath's door to keep from falling. "Derrick! You startled me," she said and laughed.

"Sorry, Derrick. She wanted to check on her horse before we went home," Jess grumbled.

"Okay, well you've seen him. He's fine. Now leave," Derrick said.

Belinda staggered toward Derrick along the wall of stalls. "Derrriick, Derrriick. What am I to do with you?" she sang.

"She's obviously drunk. You need to take her home," Derrick told Jess.

"What's your problem with me, anyway?" Belinda asked. "I just stopped by to see my horse."

Derrick turned to leave and called over his shoulder, "I don't have a problem with you, Belinda. You just have to leave, that's all. And make sure you turn off the lights and close the door on your way out."

"Wait, where are you going?" Belinda whined.

"Back to the house."

"No! You can't leave. I want to talk to you." Belinda tried to reach him, but stumbled to the ground.

Derrick looked at her and scoffed. "Another time maybe, when you're not so drunk."

"Wait!" she called. "Okay, okay, I'll go. But I need you to help me to the car. Can you do that?" She sat back on her heels.

Derrick looked from Belinda to Jess then back to Belinda. He shrugged and walked up to her. "Come on, then," he said. He hoisted her up and pulled her arm over his shoulders and wrapped his other arm around her waist.

Belinda cooed and leaned into him. He smelled shower fresh wonderful. "You smell… manly. Delicious. I could eat you up."

"That's enough, Belle," Derrick said. "Hey Jess, get the door, will you?"

Jess moved around them and opened the passenger door without comment.

Belinda clung to Derrick's neck. "Don't put me inside. Hold me." She pulled him toward her lips. "Kiss me." A crack of thunder sounded and soft rain began to fall.

Derrick reached up, took her arms, and pushed her away.

Belinda's face heated with anger and embarrassment. She gripped the bottle of rum by the neck. "Fine!" She waved the bottle. "You'll be sorry. It's your loss. Who needs you, anyway?" Liquid sloshed around and escaped to cover Derrick's shirt with stains of alcohol.

"Yeah, whatever," Derrick said, wiping at his shirt. He got on the golf cart and spun it around without another word.

"Go, then! I don't need you!"

Jess put her hand on Belinda's shoulder. "Come on, Belle. Let's get you home."

Belinda whipped away from her and turned her hatred on Jess. "Get away from me! Don't touch me!" The rain fell where tears did not.

"Belle, we can't—"

"I can do anything I want! Do you know who I am?" Belinda called, and then mumbled, "I can do anything I want." She watched Derrick in the distance park the cart by the guest house and go inside. Her eyes filled, but even in her drunken state, she refused to let any tears fall. Little Miss Casandra Rhyne would pay for turning him against her. She whirled around to Jess. "And right now I want you to drive me to the red barn."

"Come on, Belle…"

Belinda pushed past Jess and fell into the passenger seat. "Now!" she ordered and slammed the door.

Jess shook her head and rounded the front of the car to the driver's seat. "Fine. You're the boss."

As they neared the barn, Belinda slapped Jess's arm several times. "Turn the headlights off and go slow. Pull in over there between the barn and the wash stalls. There, near Derrick's truck."

Jess pulled the car halfway down the length of the barn and turned the engine off, then glared at Belinda. "Okay, genius. Now what?"

Belinda's lips curled. "I have a plan." She glanced at Jess and frowned. "Don't look at me like that. This is a beauty! Remember the auction they're doing on Wednesday at the Depot?"

Jess nodded slowly. "Aaand…"

"I'm going to make sure Arco finds his way to that auction." Belinda laughed into her hand. "Isn't it brilliant?"

Jess stared with wide eyes. "You have to be joking. Belle, that's the lowest low I've ever heard of anyone doing—even for you—and that's saying a lot. You can't be serious. Cassie hasn't done anything to you to deserve that."

Belinda looked down her nose and reached for the door. "Well, I am, and you're going to help me."

"Oh, no I'm not. There are lines you just don't cross, and this is definitely one of those lines."

"You will or I will disown you as my friend. No more free rides to the best of everything. See how you like shopping at Wal-Mart."

Jess shook her head. "Wal-Mart's just fine with me. You think I hang around with you because of your money? Maybe your head has been so far up your ass that you've failed to notice, but my family's not exactly poor. I don't need your money or your handouts."

Belinda clucked her tongue and looked away. "Fine, I'll do it myself then."

"And how do you plan on doing this?"

"Easy, I'm going to ride him through the woods to the old Miller place. No one's living there and I can keep him in the barn there until morning. I'll go back with my trailer and head to the Depot." Belinda opened the door and stepped out. She leaned in the window and smiled at Jess. "See? Perfect! Now, drive out to the main road and meet me at the Miller place. Wait for me there."

"You can't go riding out there at night," Jess scoffed. "That's just stupid. The woods are full of quicksand, especially around the Miller place. Remember?"

Belinda rolled her eyes. "Whatever, worrywart. I know my way around. Just get going and meet me there," she said, and shut the door quietly.

Belinda slid the barn door open and then waved to Jess. She slipped into the barn and stumbled her way to the tack room. Arco's bridle hung on the door of his stall. Belle stood and stared at him as he slept. How quiet he looked now. Not so tough. Though she'd never admit it to another living soul, Arco scared her. She couldn't remember the last time she'd been thrown by a horse. His shiny, pure black coat made him appear even larger than the 16.2 hands he stood.

She opened his door and patted him. "We're going for a little ride and you better behave," she said as she slid his halter from his head. She placed the bit in his mouth and moved the bridle over his ears, then led him into the aisle and hooked him to the cross-ties. Now for the saddle. Belinda scampered to the tack room and pulled the first saddle she saw.

"Stand still," she said as she struggled with the girth. She kneed his belly, gritted her teeth, and yanked harder on the girth. "And stop bloating. It's not my fault you have such wide withers. I'm not changing saddles now. This one will have to do."

Arco fidgeted forward and back.

"What's your problem, you stupid animal?" She finished saddling him and led him out of the barn, then turned the corner and waved to Jess. She walked Arco up to the green plastic mounting block and hoisted herself up onto his back.

Jess got out of the car and stared at her. "You can't do this, Belle. It isn't right. Cassie will never get over this."

"Like I should care what she feels. Does she care about me? Or what I want? She doesn't want Derrick, she just doesn't want me to have him. Do you think she cares how much that hurts me?" Belinda turned Arco toward the north field. "Now go to the Miller place and wait for me there."

"I'm not doing this," Jess said with ire. "I'm sorry, but this just isn't worth it."

"I thought you hated her as much as I do?"

Jess frowned. "I never said I hated her, and if I did, not enough to do this."

Belinda glanced back as Jess got in the car and started the engine. "I can't believe you're just going to leave me when I need you most."

To her amazement, Jess beeped the horn. Belinda froze and spun toward the guest house. Derrick appeared in the window and then was gone.

She glared back at Jess. "You idiot!" she called over her shoulder. She rammed her heels into Arco's side and he lurched forward.

Derrick ran from the porch and reached out for her. "What are you doing? Stop!"

Belinda kicked at him and he fell forward on his hands, missing them as they passed.

Derrick fumbled for his keys as he rounded the corner of the barn toward his truck. Jess stood beside her driver's door.

"Derrick, I'm so sorry. She's acting like a psycho. We have to stop her."

"My thoughts exactly. What does she think she's doing?"

"She's going to the old Miller place," Jess said. "Get in. We'll meet her there."

Derrick ran to his truck. "No, I'll head her off on Critchton Road."

"Derrick, *no.*"

###

Derrick kicked up gravel as he slammed his foot down on the gas and fishtailed away from the barn. Belinda knew she couldn't ride Arco. She'd get herself killed if he didn't stop her.

He drove out onto Brayton Street and slid on the slick, wet road. He managed to straighten the truck out and floored it. If he didn't stop her on Crichton Road, she'd be done for, and so would Arco. Cassie's warnings of quicksand flowed back to him. What was Belle thinking riding through these woods at night? It'd be suicide.

Derrick glanced down at the speedometer and wished he could go faster but the winding, wet road kept his speed at forty-five. He slowed briefly and rounded the bend that turned into Critchton Road, then increased his speed once again.

The dull wipers washed the rain over the window in a blur. The old, dark country road gleamed in front of the headlights as Derrick made his way through the night. His heart pounded and thoughts of Cassie raced through his mind.

A dark shadow sprang from the woods to the right and appeared in the middle of the road. Derrick slammed on his brakes and the small truck fishtailed out of control. Wild eyes from girl and beast flashed before him in the light. Belinda's screams mixed with his own, and then there was darkness.

CHAPTER TWO

Six Days Earlier

The whispers of the Mississippi mist swept beneath the old weeping willow tree and prickled at her neck, but Cassandra Rhyne chose to ignore them. Instead, she closed her eyes and let the blanket of warmth from the late afternoon June air caress her skin. Images of her father floated through her mind and caused teardrops to seep from the corners of her lids. *I miss you, Daddy.*

Derrick Anderson sat with his back against the deeply furrowed bark and held Cassie wrapped in the crook of his arm. He moaned and brushed his lips on the top of her head. "I'm falling asleep."

"I wish I could." Cassie gazed at the murky water of the bayou. The willow drooped gracefully out over the bank, its stem tips dancing on the still water stirring it into rippled circles.

Derrick sighed. "Come on, Cass. You have to move on. It isn't good for you to hang on to this junk. It was an accident."

Cassie pushed away and sat up. "An accident? Really, Derrick?

After everything I've told you, that's what you still believe? Well, I don't. It was murder, and I'm going to prove it."

Derrick reached out and pulled her toward him. She put up a slight resistance and then rested her head on his chest and he gently rubbed her scalp. "I'm sorry, babe. I didn't mean—"

"I can't believe you don't believe me. I'd think you of all people would be on my side."

"I know Larson's capable of a lot of things, but murder?"

"Yeah." Cassie rubbed the back of her hand down the side of her wet cheek and wiped a tear away. "I'm not crazy like everyone seems to think, and I sure don't need that shrink my mom keeps sending me to. I know what I know, and I know that man killed my father. Maybe even my Grandpa Joe, too." Cassie felt his arms tighten around her protectively.

"If that's true, then what about you?" he asked.

"Me?"

"Yeah, I mean, if someone killed your father and grandfather for their land, which has now passed to you and your mother, then…well, I mean…"

Cassie's heart picked up pace. It was a thought she hadn't considered.

"All I'm saying, Cass, is that if what you say is true, and you go poking around, then maybe that puts you and your mom in danger."

"I'm not worried about me."

"Okay, fine, then what about your mom?"

"My mom can rot for all I care."

"You don't mean that."

"Yes, I do." Cassie pushed away from him and toyed with a blade of grass. "She lied to me, Derrick."

"And so what? You're going to hold it against her for the rest of her life?"

Cassie turned a cold eye on him. "Yeah, maybe I will."

Derrick shook his head. "God, Cass, you have to learn how to forgive people. We're only human. We make mistakes. I'm sure you've made your share."

"You don't lie to someone you love."

Derrick stared deep into her. "Sometimes that's *exactly* who you lie to."

"What? Have you lied to me too?" she asked pointedly.

He softened his voice. "You haven't even forgiven your father, and it wasn't like he died on purpose."

"You don't know *anything*. You think you do, but you don't."

"Really? I can hear the anger in your voice every time you talk about him."

Cassie's eyes filled with tears. "He left me!"

Derrick pulled her closer. "I know, babe, but not because he wanted to." He kissed the top of her head. "I'm worried about you. I don't want you to get hurt."

"I told you, I don't care about me. I don't know if you've noticed, but I'm not exactly rolling in friends. My father was my best friend. No one seems to believe that he was murdered. I'm the only one who knows and that means it's up to me to prove it, at whatever cost. So, I really don't care what happens to me in the process."

"Well, I do."

He squeezed her shoulders and she snuggled closer to the safety of his arms. Deep down inside, she had to admit, she was terrified.

"I guess I just want a better explanation to what happened to my dad. It's hard for me to believe a six-foot-three, strong swimmer like him drowned in five feet of water." She tilted her face up to his.

"I know you do." Derrick sighed. "We all want a better explanation, really. And I promise, I will do whatever it takes to help you prove it. But…"

"But?" Cassie asked.

"But I think you should be prepared in case we can't prove it was murder."

She flinched and his grip tightened.

"What I mean is," he continued, "maybe it really was just a terrible accident."

Cassie pinched her lips together and then resigned from the argument. "Yeah, maybe."

An hour passed in silence beneath the willow tree. Cassie stirred first and Derrick gave her a gentle nudge. "You still awake?" he asked.

"Mm hmm," she whispered. "But the beat of your heart is close to putting me out."

"I just caught myself in a snooze," he said.

"We can't both fall asleep, or one of us might lose a leg." She laughed and poked him in the side.

Derrick sat up a little straighter. "Wow. I didn't think of that. Good point."

Cassie pushed herself up, too. "I'll make a Southerner out of you yet."

"But wouldn't the horses let us know if an alligator crept up on the bank?"

Cassie glanced over at Arco and Dillon grazing in the open field. "Yeah, I suppose they would…by their sudden galloping away!" They both laughed.

"You're very lucky, you know," Derrick said.

"Yeah, right, I'm covered in it."

Derrick glanced around, waving his hand at the beautiful expanse. "Look at all this. Do you have any idea how many people would love to live like this?"

Cassie looked out at the green open fields where the horses grazed beneath the oak trees, the Spanish moss swaying gently above them. The warm scent of swamp flowers, algae, and moss drifted through the air. She guessed it was sort of picturesque.

"And the bayou; can you smell that?" he continued.

"No, what?"

He leaned his head back and crinkled his nose. "Candy…or maybe lemon? Weird."

"I think you're smelling the magnolias." She pointed. "See those trees over there with the big white flowers and thick green leaves along the side of the lane? They're the Mississippi state flower. I guess I'm so used to it that I don't smell them anymore."

"That's too bad." He sighed and then took and exaggerated inhale. "I hope I never become immune to this."

Cassie laughed. "Derrick, you sound like a creepy romantic."

He tickled her side with his finger. "I am a romantic, lucky for you."

She turned her face up to his and he gave her a quick peck on the lips.

"Anyway, where I come from, this sort of place only exists in books," he said.

"You've lived here for six months; I'd think you'd be used to it by now."

"Nah, not really. I still appreciate each day for what it is." His voice lowered. "You never know when it will be your last."

"What was it like in Boston?" Cassie asked, missing his last statement.

Derrick shrugged. "A city. Just like New York, and Chicago, and San Francisco. Just... cities."

"You've never lived in the suburbs before?"

"Nope, only cities."

"That must have been exciting. I'd like to go to a real city sometime. Hit the high road, if you know what I mean."

"City living's not all everyone makes it out to be," he said. "And the schools suck."

"You mean they're worse than ours? That's hard to believe."

"Yeah, a lot worse. Lots of sex, drugs, and rock 'n roll, as they say." He flashed a cool smirk. "I'm not much into drugs or alcohol, but the sex and rock 'n roll weren't too bad."

Cassie's eyes widened in mock surprise and she poked him hard. "Nice! Not exactly what your girlfriend wants to hear."

Derrick laughed and tugged her in. "It was just fun. Nothing real."

Cassie gazed up at him but didn't speak. The thought of him with other girls tugged at her gut. "But you're mine now," she whispered.

He cupped her face in both his hands and stared into her eyes and nodded. "You're the real thing," he breathed.

Cassie's body folded into him. Even if she lived a thousand years, she'd never get over the feelings he stirred inside her every time they kissed. Her heartbeat thudded in her ears, her palms sweat, and her body tingled. Each gentle touch reached inside and set loose a hundred butterflies within her.

His gaze fell to her mouth and his tongue darted out to wet his lips. His breaths became ragged.

Cassie's body weakened and she leaned more heavily into him. "Kiss me," she murmured. "Before I explode."

And he did.

Fierce passion raged between them as if each competed for consumption of the other.

Derrick's hands glided down her sides to the bottom of her t-shirt and fumbled to pull it up. Their lips still locked, Cassie inched her body away to give him room to lift it off.

A whisper rode the breeze to her ear. *Secrets.*

Cassie stopped his hands. "Wait, Derrick, not here."

He lifted his head. Gold specks flickered in his marble green eyes. "Wow."

"I'm sorry, it's just—"

"No, don't be. I mean wow that was amazing."

Cassie chuckled, still attempting to catch her breath. "I know what you mean."

He rubbed his nose against hers and smiled. "I love you."

Cassie stiffened and her mind raced for words. Did she need to say them back? Did she even feel the same?

"Well?"

"Well what?" she asked.

"Wwweell?"

That answers that question, she thought. "Oh! Yeah. I love you, too."

Derrick tilted his head and squinted. "Good...I think." He didn't press it, much to her relief, but stood and held his hand out to help her up.

"What are you doing?" she asked.

"I have to get going. I told my mom I'd be home by six for dinner and it's almost five. We still have to put the horses away."

"Yeah, you're right." The next thought made Cassie roll her eyes and snarl her lips. "I almost forgot that I'm supposed to help Mom with Belinda's riding lesson tonight."

"I didn't know she was coming by tonight. What time?"

Cassie cast a small pout and moved away. "Her lesson is at seven. Why so interested?"

"Maybe I'll come and watch," Derrick teased.

Cassie spun around and faced him. "That's not funny, Derrick. I don't like you flirting with the enemy. It's like you want to lead her on or something...unless you really are interested?"

"Come on, Cass, I was only joking. I don't flirt with her and you know it so you can put the ugly away."

Cassie continued to pout. "She *is* prettier than me."

"In your eyes only."

Cassie's cheeks warmed and she moved away. "Anyway, I'm sure your mother won't mind if you stay for dinner."

Derrick's eyes clouded.

"Wait, you think she'd mind? Doesn't she like me?" Cassie's skin prickled, and for the briefest of moments panic fell heavy on her chest.

Derrick gave her a weak smile. "It's not you. She loves you. It's me she doesn't love much anymore."

Cassie breathed a sigh of relief. "Why would you say that? She's your mother; she sort of has to love you."

Derrick picked up the bridle, walked to Dillon, and lifted his head up by the halter. He threw the reins over Dillon's head and gently pushed the bit into his mouth. "Yeah, she used to love me, but now she only loves me because she's my mother; it's nothing more than that. There *is* a difference that can be felt, you know?" He moved to Dillon's side, stuck his foot in the stirrup, and mounted in one swift motion.

A wave of lust rushed over her. He'd learned to handle a horse like a pro in less than six months; he was a natural. She looked away to focus on the conversation. "You're just being paranoid. She loves you with her whole heart. I'm sure of it."

Derrick stared at Cassie long and hard as if he was about to speak, then smiled and faced Dillon in the direction of Cassie's home. "If we're going to race, you better get aboard," he said, and trotted off down the oak tree lined, dirt covered path of Willow Tree Lane.

Cassie hopped on Arco and cantered up to him. They pulled their horses into a walk. "Is that why you won't ask me over? I mean, we've been dating for two months and I've only really spoken to your parents like, twice. You practically live at my house."

"Drop it, will you?"

"I'm sorry. I'm just curious, that's all. I mean, most parents suck. Yours aren't that bad," she said with a smile.

She wished Derrick's relationship with his parents was better, but they seemed to be always at odds with each other, always tugging and pulling. Sometimes Cassie thought they resented her relationship with him. She didn't know why, exactly, but it was important for his parents to like her. She cringed at the thought of being the cause of any friction between them and Derrick.

Derrick furrowed his eyebrows and stared straight ahead. "Maybe they're embarrassed of me. I haven't exactly been a golden child."

"Come on. What could you have done that would change how they feel about you?" Something stirred in her stomach and a wave of uneasiness spread within. What was that word she heard on the wind while they kissed?

The breeze picked up and tiny prickles crawled up Cassie's spine. She attempted to shrug it off.

Secrets, the winds from the bayou whispered again. *Ask him.*

Derrick glanced at her without speaking.

"Hey, you hiding something?" Cassie asked reluctantly.

Derrick remained silent a moment too long. "Hiding?" He shook his head. "Some things need a little more time to tell, that's all."

CHAPTER THREE

Katherine Rhyne appeared in the living room carrying a tray of coffee and sweet biscuits. She nodded toward the sofa. "Please, Frank, make yourself at home."

Frank Larson pushed aside the big brown and teal pillows on the chocolate-colored, over-stuffed sofa and sat in the middle. He tossed his black Stetson on the coffee table, stretched his arms out across the back, and rested his ankle on his knee. A broad grin crossed his face and Kate couldn't help but think how she'd like to wipe it from him. Her smile hid her disdain for the man who sat just feet away.

Kate sat in the wing-backed chair and set the tray on the coffee table, brushing aside Frank's hat. "May I pour you a coffee?"

"Tell you the truth, I'd much prefer a shot of whiskey."

Kate nodded and rose. "I believe I have a bottle here somewhere." She walked to the liquor cabinet behind the sofa and rummaged around. "I have some Kentucky bourbon. Will that do?"

"That'll do just fine."

A moment later, Kate returned with the drink and placed it on the coaster in front of Frank. "So what brings you by? I wasn't expecting to see you until Tuesday at the lawyer's office."

Frank leaned forward and picked up his drink, drank it down in a shot, wiped his mouth with the back of his hand, and then set the glass down on the table beside the coaster. "Something's come up that I wanted to speak with you about first."

Kate eyed his drink glass with annoyance while she poured herself a coffee. "Oh?"

Frank cleared his throat. "I have a new proposition for you, Kate. It appears my original plans have changed somewhat."

"Oh, Frank, I'm so glad. We really don't need a strip mall in—"

"Now, hold on. I never said I was building a strip mall. That's a conclusion you and your late husband jumped to. I just let it ride."

Kate didn't move or speak. Instead, she held her breath.

"I need more land, Katherine."

"For what, if not a mall?"

"I'm afraid I'm not at liberty to say at this time."

"Then no."

"Now, hear me out. You'll have a stake in this. I'm willing to give you two percent of profits for two years."

Kate placed her cup and saucer down on the coffee table harder than she meant to. "Frank, you've got to be kidding. My husband hasn't been dead for more than six months, and you're acting like a vulture on his carcass. You're a City Councilman, for crying out loud, and running for mayor. As it stands now, if you were to get elected, you'd own nearly the whole town."

Frank chuckled. "Nearly, Katherine, but not all."

"You don't need our land. My husband inherited this land from his father, who inherited it from his father. Now it belongs to Cassie. My husband turned part of this land into an equestrian center to fulfill Cassie's dream. I'm never going sell out to you."

"I didn't ask for all of it, at least not yet." He snickered. "Just ten more acres will do just fine. And don't underestimate me. It's not a question of *if* I get elected, it's *when*. There's a lot of money here, as you know from the people that board those expensive horses in your barns and pay for those expensive lessons you give. I just want to give the people what they need. A few shopping centers with high end stores, restaurants, and maybe even a kiddie park or two. Named after me, of course." Frank winked with a smirk.

Kate stared down at the coffee cup on the table. "There's more to life than money, Frank."

Frank leaned back on the sofa and grinned. "This coming from you? I would think you'd jump at the chance. If it wasn't for my initial deal, you'd be selling a lot more than a few acres. I heard you have four more horses ready for the auction next week. How many is that now, eight?"

Anger and embarrassment crawled up Kate's skin. "It's true, I've been selling some horses, yes. But it doesn't mean—"

Frank held up his hand to stop her. "I know your financial status and I know you need this. Come on, Katherine, you won't find a better deal than what I'm offering you right now."

Kate rose and moved across the room. She stared out the bay window and watched Cassie and Derrick gallop down Willow Tree

Lane. Her stomach tightened. Cassie would never forgive her if she continued to sell the land to Larson. "I know your offer is a good one," she finally said, "but I'm just not prepared to sell off so much of my daughter's land. I don't even want to sell the thirty-five acres we've already agreed on, but you're right, I have to." She faced him with a stoic stance. "I'm sorry, Frank. The answer is no."

Frank shook his head and sighed. He leaned forward, his face serious, and picked up his Stetson, tapping it against his hand. A moment passed, and then he glanced up at Kate and smiled. He rose slowly and moved toward the door, his boots falling heavy on the hardwood floor. "I hope you won't regret this decision. I mean, there's always the possibility I could find the land I need from the Ashcroft estate on the other side of the Miller plantation. And as you know, I have the Miller place tied up in litigation. Those two properties together might give me just what I need. If things go my way—as I anticipate they will—well, then I just won't be able to help you out any more than I already have." He nodded.

Kate crossed her arms and tilted her head. "Are you threatening me, Mr. Councilman?"

"Threatening? Nah, that's a harsh word. I'm a businessman, Mrs. Rhyne, that's all. I'm merely suggesting you consider this deal...for your own good, of course."

A large form of a man appeared in the arched doorway to the kitchen. He leaned casually against the door frame and slowly wiped down a glass with a white dish towel. "You all right, ma'am?" he asked.

Kate glanced at her ranch foreman and that back to Frank. "Yes,

Noah, I'm fine. Thank you. Mr. Larson was just leaving."

Noah continued to dry the glass with a slow and steady motion. He stared at Frank with narrowed eyes. "I'd be happy to assist, ma'am." The deeply etched lines of his face made him appear as a wise elder, but the rest of Noah Hickman didn't give a hint to his age. Slender and tall, standing straight two inches over six feet, the muscles of his shoulders and arms were that of a fifty-year-old man. The elderly hunch had yet to catch up to his sixty-four-year-old body.

Kate held the door open.

Frank stepped into the doorway. "Easy there, young 'fella," he joked to Noah.

Kate continued to hold the door open. "I'm not afraid of you, Frank. Neither you nor your lawyer friends can force me to sell off more than I want to. Now, if you'll excuse me, I have work to do."

Frank Larson stepped out onto the porch and squinted up at the late afternoon sun. He placed his hat on his head and stepped briskly down the steps. "All right, Katherine. All right. But you just give it some thought, that's all I ask." He rounded his truck and glanced toward the lane as Cassie and Derrick thundered up to them, laughing. "Mornin', Miss Cassie," he said and tapped the rim of his hat with a nod. "That's a beautiful animal you got there." He winked with a mischievous grin. "Wanna sell him?"

Cassie's smile slipped away. "Not to a scumbag like you."

"Cassandra," Kate scolded.

Frank gave a sturdy laugh. "I didn't think so. You should enjoy him for as long as you can. You never know when troubled times might come along."

Kate and Noah walked out onto the porch as Frank climbed into his truck.

Frank glanced over at Kate and continued to smile. "And troubles always come along." He slid in behind the wheel and called out the passenger window as he shoved the truck in gear, "Gotta run. My wife will be bringing my daughter by for her lesson after dinner. Around seven, I think. Make sure you work her hard. The girl's not afraid of hard work," he said as he turned his truck around and drove away.

The dirt lane wound the three-quarter mile between the two white-fenced pastures that led to the main road. Oak trees with thick hanging moss arched over the lane and cast dark shadows beneath. They all stood silently as the dust from the large, silver Ford F450 rose in the air, hiding the truck like a magician's cloak. Kate raised her hand to her throat. When the dust settled, the truck was gone, but the bitter taste of trepidation lingered in the air. A gentle breeze whispered beneath Kate's shoulder-length brown hair and tickled at her earlobe. She gazed out in the distance at the bright, cloudless summer sky and shivered.

CHAPTER FOUR

Noah stood by the refrigerator. "I'm finished for the evening, ma'am. If there's nothing else, I'll be heading home now."

Kate smiled. "That's fine, Noah, thanks. And thanks for your offer to help with Mr. Larson."

"My pleasure, ma'am."

Kate gazed at him a long moment with a faint smile. "I don't know how we'd manage around here without you. You're a good friend, Noah."

Noah shifted and a small smiled tugged at the corner of his mouth.

Cassie set the dinner plates down on the table and grinned. "Agreed. Noah's my buds, aren't you, Noah?"

He nodded and moved toward the door.

Cassie giggled at his bashfulness.

Derrick touched her arm. "I have to head home, too, I'm already late. I'll be here in the morning, early. Promise." He leaned down and brushed a kiss to her lips, then followed Noah out.

The front door clicked a moment later. Cassie observed Kate stirring the pot on the stove. "Mom, are you all right?"

"Hmm? Oh, fine, honey," Kate replied. "Let's just have a nice dinner, hmm?"

The nice dinner consisted of beef stew, potatoes, carrots, and quiet. Cassie glanced up to speak once or twice, but the furrowed brows on her mother's face made her hold her tongue. When they'd finished, both rose and cleared the table with continued silence.

Cassie cleared her throat. "Care to tell me what that was all about? Or why Larson was here in the first place?"

"Nothing to worry about. Just business," Kate answered.

Cassie huffed. "We shouldn't be doing business with those people."

"Sometimes it's unavoidable."

Cassie squinted at Kate. "Mom, is there something going on that I don't know about? I mean, I thought we had a pact of no more secrets between us."

"I'm not hiding anything, honey." Kate's smile didn't reach her eyes. "You know we've been struggling lately with some bills and that I've had to sell some horses. Well, I've decided to sell a few more acres to Mr. Larson to help us over the hill."

"More property? You're selling that murdering bastard more of Dad's property? God, Mom, if you keep this up you might as well sell him the whole stinking farm."

"Let's not get all melodramatic." Kate tsked as she dropped the dishes into the sink and started washing. "You have to stop saying that kind of stuff, Cassie. And we still have plenty of land."

Cassie pulled the towel from the stove and dried what Kate put on the counter. "Let me guess, he wants more."

"It doesn't mean he's going to get more." Kate leaned on the sink and looked at Cassie. "Now, can you give me a break and drop it?"

Cassie pressed her back against the sink as she absentmindedly continued to wipe a glass. "He killed Dad, you know."

Kate let out a long, tense breath. "Cassie, we've been through this a thousand times. Mr. Larson has been cleared of any wrongdoing in your father's death. Don't you think if I thought for one second that he had anything to do with it that I would do everything in my power to bring him down? It was an accident." Kate returned her focus to the dishes in the sink. "A terrible accident."

Cassie leaned on the counter next to her mother, steadied her thoughts, and chose each word with care before she spoke. "Yeah, Mom, I know you would…if you believed. They're all wrong, the doctors, the coroner, all of them. The spirits of the mist told me the truth and I'm going to—"

Kate slammed her hands down on the edge of the sink and closed her eyes. "Dammit, girl, will you stop this nonsense?" Her angry eyes met Cassie's. "What are you trying to do, get yourself locked away in some psych hospital? I lost your father and now this? There are no spirits in the mist! It was a game your grandfather and father played with you. That's all. Nothing more. You have to stop this."

Cassie shoved off the counter and walked away from her. "It isn't nonsense," she called over her shoulder, "and it wasn't a game. The mist does speak to me, just as it did to Grandpa Joe and just as it did to Dad." She spun around with a glare. "You would hear them too, if you'd only listen." Her voice rose to a small squeal. "And I'm *not* crazy."

Kate's expression changed so suddenly that Cassie recoiled from the sorrow in her eyes.

"I don't think you're crazy, sweetheart, just under a lot of stress and—"

Cassie spun away from her and cut her off with a wave of her hand. "Whatever."

She finished drying the dishes and placed the last of the glasses in the cupboard. "Is it okay if I get Sampson ready for Belle's lesson now?"

Kate sighed. "Thanks, honey. That would be great."

###

Cassie stepped out on the porch and looked at the golf cart parked near the steps, then up at the star-filled sky. The night cooled the afternoon heat somewhat, but the humidity remained.

"I'm not crazy," she said to the stars. She looked out past the north pasture into the black bayou. "It wasn't just a game, was it?"

A faint breeze floated beneath her ear. *Not a game.*

"Then tell me what to do. How can I prove that Larson murdered my dad? No one believes me."

Nothing.

"Please answer me. I can't do this without you."

Again, nothing.

"I need you, Daddy," Cassie whispered.

A gentle whisper swirled past her ear. *When the time is right.*

Cassie smiled and stepped off the porch. She climbed into the cart and drove the quarter mile up to the indoor arena, pulled the cart into the barn, and parked on the long cement alleyway in front of Sampson's stall where he greeted her with a soft whinny.

"Hey, big boy. I have something for you." She dug out a bag of carrots from under the back seat of the cart. "You didn't think I'd forget, did you?" She pulled a long carrot from the bag, grasped it in her hand, and let him bite off half.

"Time for some exercise. You're in for a real treat tonight. Belle's coming to ride you." Her fingers tickled his muzzle. "I know, I know. Treat my butt. But I'm sure you'll do fine. Just don't take any of her bull, all right? Stand up for yourself this time."

Cassie walked Sampson from his stall, around the front of the building, and then entered the long paved hall parallel to the arena. She hooked him to the cross-ties, went to the tack room and pulled his saddle and bridle from the rack on the wall, picked up the grooming bucket, and then returned to prep him for the lesson.

Her mind drifted to her conversation with her mother at dinner as she brushed him. *Nothing to worry about*, her mother had said. That usually meant there was plenty to worry about. Cassie frowned. The word around town was that business with Frank Larson always meant trouble of some sort. He had a reputation for bullying and was known for throwing his weight around. Rumor had it that he even had the sheriff in his pocket. But Cassie tended to doubt that. She'd known Sheriff Winslow for a long time. His daughter Jessica had been her best friend all the way from third grade up until last year's fallout. Now they were ex-best friends. Again Cassie grimaced. It didn't take long for Jess to disown her and start groveling at the feet of Belinda

Larson. Jess and Belle quickly became best friends, and Cassie became the outcast. Just another perfect reason to despise Belle.

She finished tightening Sampson's girth, then unclipped him from the cross-ties and led him down the aisle toward the arena. His hoof beats echoed down the paved hall under the high ceiling until the deep sand of the arena silenced them. She reached for one of the lunge whips from the wall as they entered. They walked out to the middle of the arena where she clipped the reins to the sides of the saddle, and then hooked the lunge line to the bridle. She let him out and gently coaxed him into a trot by shaking the long whip behind him.

Cassie worked Sampson for fifteen minutes tracking left, and then reversed for another fifteen. "Tk, tk, easy boy," she said, and slowed him to a stop. She walked up to him and patted his sweaty neck. "I know it's hot. I wish you didn't have to work tonight. Maybe she'll only want a half hour instead of a full. Remember how she complains about the grossness of sweating?" She snuggled against his face and chuckled.

Voices drifted through the barn, soft at first, and then Cassie heard the nasty shrill of Belle's sarcasm as they drew closer. A moment later, she appeared in the doorway to the arena.

Belinda and her mother, Ruth Ann, entered in front of Kate. Belinda pouted and stomped over to Cassie and Sampson. "This poor thing again? Really?"

"There's nothing wrong with him," Cassie said.

"How old is this poor creature?" Belle continued.

Cassie glanced at Kate and Kate rolled her eyes, and then looked away. Cassie glared at Belle. "Stop that. He's not a poor thing, he's a champion."

"Maybe at one time, but look at him. His head nearly drags the ground. He looks like an old hag."

"Now, Belinda, he seems fine for a lesson horse. You did well on him your last few rides," Ruth Ann said.

"You think? I nearly killed him!" Belle said. "I can't wait for Goliath to get back from training."

Cassie turned and headed toward the side rail with Sampson. "If you don't want to ride him, you don't have to. All the better for him."

Belle stomped up to Cassie and took the reins away from her. "If I must ride this poor creature, then let's just do it."

Cassie moved to stop her, but Kate stepped forward. "Cassie, would you mind taking Mrs. Larson up to the observatory and getting her something to drink?" Kate smiled and nodded. "Thank you, sweetheart."

Cassie paused and clenched her jaw. "Sure. No problem." She walked to Ruth Ann and smiled. "I put a pitcher of fresh sweet tea in the refrigerator this morning when Mom told me you'd be coming out tonight."

"You're such a dear," Ruth Ann said with a gentle smile.

Cassie couldn't help wondering how such a nice woman like Ruth Ann Larson could have wound up with the devil's servant as a husband and then spawned a childlike Belle.

Once Mrs. Larson was settled in the observatory, Cassie returned downstairs to the side rail and watched the lesson. Her blood boiled every time Belle tugged, kicked, yanked, whipped, and jabbed Sampson unnecessarily—which, in Cassie's opinion, was most of the time. She wanted to walk up to Belle and rip her off Sampson, and she even attempted to enter the ring once or twice, but Kate froze her with her evil eye.

When the lesson ended forty-five minutes later, a winded Belle dismounted and handed the sweaty Sampson to Cassie with a smile. "Not bad, for an old 'has been.' When Goliath gets back from training in California, you'll see what a real horse can do."

Cassie's face heated with anger. She clenched her teeth and lowered her voice. "You have no idea—"

"Cassie, honey, why don't you walk Sampson out, and then hose him down?" Kate smiled.

"But, Mom—" Cassie started, but Kate's eyes affirmed her suggestion wasn't a request. Cassie huffed. "Fine." She shot the smirking Belle a scowl and shoved past her, followed by a very tired Sampson, still puffing, his head low. Cassie patted Sampson's neck. "I'm sorry, big guy. I'll make sure she never rides you again. I can't believe Mom didn't stop the lesson. I don't understand what's so special about these people."

Belle ran out and caught up to Cassie and Sampson. "Hey, wait up."

Cassie continued walking, whispering to the horse.

"Hey, I said wait," Belle said, and grabbed Cassie's arm.

Cassie spun toward her. "What?"

"Oh, sorry, did I interrupt one of your special moments with the voices in your head?" Belle slapped her hand against her thigh and laughed out loud. "I crack me up."

Cassie rolled her eyes and continued walking.

Belle shrugged. "You're the one who told everyone you hear voices, not me. Remember? You said the swamp voices talk to you." She reached out and grabbed Cassie's arm again. "And we're not supposed to think you're crazy?" She let go and moved toward Sampson. "Anyway, once Goliath gets here, I'll be here nearly every night. I have to keep up my training for the fall competition in Biloxi."

"And what? You want to be friends or something?"

Belle laughed. "Don't be silly. We can't be friends, you work for me." She flipped her long blond hair with her finger and gave Cassie a look up and down, then wrinkled her nose. "Besides, I couldn't be seen with someone who doesn't even know how to dress in the current fashions." She signed and tossed her hair again, with a jerk of her head. "But Mother says we all can't be fortunate." Peering down at the horse, she smiled. "So I guess I'll be riding this old boy a couple more times."

"Oh, no, you won't. You're not riding him again. Ever!" Cassie snarled. "Hear me?"

Belle smiled. "Of course I will. I can ride any horse I choose." She cocked her head with a squint in her eye. "Maybe I'll choose…that one," she said, and pointed to a horse sticking his head out of his stall. "The Friesian there. I've watched you ride him, though I have to say, you don't do him much justice. He seems like he could be a good mover."

Cassie clenched her fists. "Arco is not one of the lesson horses, he's mine. You can't ride him."

"Hmpf. Didn't you hear what I said? I can ride anyone I choose. I think I'll go tell your mother that I want to ride him right now." She flashed a smirk and flipped her hair with a shake of her head.

"You do and you're dead. Arco isn't used to other people. You couldn't manage him," Cassie hissed. "If I didn't kill you, he would."

Mrs. Larson honked her horn and waved.

"Ah, saved by the bell, so to speak," Belle said, and laughed.

Cassie stared at Belle's back as she sauntered off toward her mother under the moonlit sky. A smile slowly crossed her face. On second thought, maybe it wouldn't be such a bad idea to let her ride Arco. Maybe he'd teach her a lesson. Maybe, just maybe, she'd be rid of her once and for all.

CHAPTER FIVE

Derrick woke to the sound of the garbage truck and squeezed his pillow over his head. Why, for the love of God, did they have to pick up trash at seven a.m. on a Saturday? He lay still, trying to force himself back to sleep, but the voices coming from the downstairs kitchen and the strong smell of coffee stirred his senses into full gear.

He slithered from his bed and shivered against the cold, air-conditioned air. His father complained about the electric bill, yet he kept the house at a cool sixty-eight degrees. It was his mother's doing. She'd been suffering hot flashes for the past year, driving Derrick and his father nuts with her mood swings. They'd both decided it was better to freeze themselves out than to watch her fan herself like a swooning Southern Belle while cussing up a storm. Derrick slid into a pair of jeans he picked up from the end of the bed, grabbed a t-shirt from the floor, smelled it, and then threw it over his shoulder.

He left his room and caught sight of his father at the top of the stair landing heading toward his bedroom with a newspaper under his arm.

"You weren't going in there, were you?" Doug Anderson chortled, pointing at the bathroom door.

Derrick glanced at the newspaper and knew it had been a long stay. "Nope. I'm good. I showered last night before bed. I'll brush my teeth in the downstairs bathroom."

"Good idea," Doug said and chuckled on his way to his room.

Derrick bounded down the stairs and pushed through the swinging doors into the kitchen. "Hey, Mom," he said as he grabbed a Toaster Strudel from the freezer.

"Derrick, let me make you something more than that to eat."

"No time. I have to get to Cassie's and help her do turn-outs this morning."

Cori poured him a cup of coffee and placed it on the table. "Derrick, I think you've been spending too much time there, at the Rhynes'. I mean, you're not even supposed to be driving unless it's for work purposes."

Derrick rolled his eyes and scoffed. "It is for work purposes. I'm working on the farm, remember? And besides, don't you think Dad should be over the driving restrictions by now? I've proved myself over and over but he doesn't seem to care."

The toaster popped and Cori leaned past Derrick to remove the pastry. "I know, but the accident—"

"Was more than a freaking year ago. Are you people ever going to let it go, or are you going to make me pay for it for the rest of my life?"

Cori's voice rose with indignation. "No one's making you pay for anything."

"Really? I'm seventeen and have a 'before dark' curfew, I can't drive my own car unless it's for work or school, and I'm not allowed to have a girlfriend. What would you call it?"

"We never said you couldn't have a girlfriend."

"How am I supposed to have a girlfriend when I can't ever spend time with her?" Derrick jumped to his feet and shoved the chair back, nearly tipping it over. "You know what? Forget it. I'm going to Cassie's...*to work*," he said, and left through the side door off the kitchen so he wouldn't chance running into his father.

"Derrick, wait. *Derrick*."

"Tell the Gestapo leader that I'll be home for dinner," he said, and slammed the door of the rusted pale blue Mazda pickup. His mother stood in the doorway as he backed out of the driveway, and his gut wrenched. Would they ever forgive him? Would her fear ever end? Would he ever feel her love again?

He jammed the gear in drive and pressed his foot on the gas, causing the tires to screech as he drove away. The hell with it. It didn't matter, anyway. No one could hate him anymore than he already hated himself. As far as he was concerned, he was a short-timer in this life. If it wasn't for Cassie, he'd already have checked out. But he couldn't do that to her, not after she just lost her father. His mouth dried. Once Cassie found out his secret, she'd hate him too, and then what little purpose he had to his life would be gone forever.

But for now, until that day, he'd live for her.

CHAPTER SIX

Cassie finished mucking out the last two stalls of the lower barn and then drove the golf cart with the small wagon in tow to the manure pile. She glanced toward the upper barn and watched as Noah pulled around back with the manure spreader. A small tinge of jealousy pricked her skin. He got the manure spreader, while she got to do double the work filling and emptying the wagon.

She finished piling up the manure, then returned to the lower barn and parked in front of the center aisle. The large black and white industrial clock above the vending machine read eight-fifteen. A smile creased her lips. Early Saturday mornings apparently weren't Derrick's strong suit.

Movement out by the west field made Cassie turn just in time to see her mother release Hero and Shiloh into the pasture and close the gate. Kate leaned on the rail and smiled at the two magnificent creatures as they tossed their heads from side to side and galloped away, their manes and tails dancing in the wind behind them.

Kate turned in Cassie's direction and raised her hand to shield her eyes from the morning sun. Cassie waved and Kate waved back. Cassie saddened. All she'd ever needed to make the world a livable place was a smile and a hug from her mother. But when her father died, Kate's smiles and hugs died too, at least for a while. It was during that time that Cassie needed them most, but Kate was dealing with her own demons and Cassie felt abandoned.

Her mind flooded with thoughts of her mother's betrayal, lies, and deceit, and anger replaced her sadness. She unhooked the wagon from the cart with annoyance and then chided herself. "Dammit, girl, you need to get over this. She did what she thought was best. And all this anger isn't very Christian. Forgiveness will set you free, remember?"

She observed Kate as she walked up the long road toward the lower barn. "I do forgive her…most of the time," she mumbled. She got in the cart and headed down to pick up her mother. *But you know the truth.* Cassie frowned and shrugged it away. "Stop," she said to the open air. "I don't need you to tell me what I already know."

"What a great morning, huh?" Kate asked as Cassie pulled up beside her. "You couldn't ask for a better one for June." She looked up at the clear blue sky and bright yellow sphere and chortled. "But it's going to be a screamer as the day goes on. We need to make sure we check the electronic waterers in the upper barn. They've been acting up a bit lately."

"Right. Dad wanted to buy those Bar-Bar-A automatic horse drinkers for the barns, remember? He said they'd work better."

Kate's smile softened. "I know, but one thing at a time. The barns already had the electronic systems in place. But now that they're acting up, I just might give the Bar-Bar-A a call."

They both turned at the sound of the old dinner bell.

Kate patted Cassie's leg. "Okay, now let's go get some breakfast."

Cassie pulled up to the old 1800s two story plantation house where Clara, the housekeeper, stood smiling, flashing the whitest teeth Cassie had ever seen. Derrick said they appeared whiter because of her dark skin, but Cassie'd studied those teeth for the past few years and they were as white as snow, dark skin or not.

Clara had one hand in her apron, the other wrapped around one of the white columns that traced the length of the porch on either side of the steps. She leaned forward against the white picket-style railing between the columns and chuckled. "Breakfast is on. You ladies must be fit fo' eatin' aft'a all that they'a hard work."

Cassie smiled at the woman's thick Southern accent. "Starving, Clara. I hope you made enough to feed a small army."

Clara patted Cassie's shoulder as she walked past into the house. "Ya sayin', but ya nev'a eat more than a mouthful."

Kate laughed as she ascended the steps. "I know, right? Tell her for me. She needs some fattening up."

Cassie jerked around to rebut, then saw Kate pause at the doorway and pick a chip of yellow paint from the house. Kate backed away and looked it over from left to right. "Well, that paint job didn't last long. Remind me to get with Noah on this, will you, Clara?"

"Yes'um," Clara said.

Cassie leaned out the doorway and glanced to her right. "Since you're checking out the house, did you happen to notice that wasp's nest being built behind that shutter?"

"No!" Kate said. "I hate bees, and wasps even more. When were you going to tell me? When they had a whole resort built?"

"Sorry, I meant to, but just kept forgetting." Guilt touched her heart. The wasps had been building for over a week, but this was yet another of her silent punishments for her mother's betrayal. She turned back into the house and mumbled, "Sorry."

Cassie ambled down the hallway toward the guest bathroom. "I'll wash and meet you in the kitchen," she said without looking back.

Three bedrooms lined the hallway on either side, and she glanced in each room as she passed, half expecting to see Grandpa Joe sitting on one of the beds. It was no secret that she'd hated the idea of moving into this house after his death two years earlier, but her father had claimed that it was for the best. Cassie disagreed, just for the record.

Grandpa Joe's passing had left a hole in her heart. But the more she'd learned of his sudden death, the more she felt something terrible had happened to him. His death didn't make sense. Her father told her mother so. And when they'd come for his funeral service, the spirits in the mist were restless. Had he become one of them? Was his spirit also disturbed?

Just as her father and Grandpa Joe had agreed, her father had quickly settled into getting the property in order to build part of it into an equestrian center. Partly, Cassie thought, to take his mind off of his loss, and partly to fulfill his promise to his father.

His eyes gleamed when he said he'd make this home her castle. It was their project, their father/daughter time, their bonding time. All she ever wanted to do was to please him as much as he pleased her. She was his princess; he always said so.

It had taken less than the year her father had estimated to get Rhyne Farms Equestrian Center up and running. They had their first boarder exactly eleven months and two days after they'd moved in—three days before Thanksgiving. And exactly five months, three days, twelve hours, and thirty-seven minutes after that evening of celebration, her world went gray, the castle dark. Her father was gone. Now she'd become a prisoner in this over-sized dungeon. She wanted nothing more than to escape...and find the truth about her father. It was a terrible accident, they said. He fell from his boat and banged his head, knocking him out, they said. They'd found him face down in the swampy water. He'd drowned, they said. They lied. The police, the coroner, the neighbors, and Kate—all liars. Accident? No way. He was murdered. The swamp whisperers said so, and now it was up to her to prove it.

Cassie gritted her teeth as she pulled the pale pink towel from the gold ring on the wall. She stared into the mirror but it was her father's face that stared back. "Why can't she believe in me the way you did?"

She laid the towel on the sink and then walked down the hall and paused at the second door on the right. Grandpa Joe's room. She stepped inside and sat on his bed. "I miss you, Grandpa Joe." Cassie lifted the small black leather-bound book from the oak night stand and stared down at the gold embossed letters of the Holy Bible. She laid a careful palm on the cover and prayed. "I know you're with me, Lord. You've helped me through so much already. But I have to ask for more. Please help me through my anger. Help me to trust my mother again. I miss what we used to have. I want it like it was when my father was alive. I've forgiven you for taking him, why can't I forgive her for lying to me about it?"

"Cassie?" Her mother's voice trailed down the hall.

Cassie quickly replaced the Bible on the night stand. "Coming."

Kate stood at the end of the hall. "You all right, honey?"

Cassie gave her weak smile. "Fine, Mom." She glanced at Kate as she passed by her into the kitchen and wondered if her mother ever knew how close she'd come to losing her daughter.

Someone knocked on the front door and Kate answered it.

"Look who's here," Kate said.

Cassie's heart leapt and a smile broke out across her face at the sound of his voice.

"Hi, Mrs. Rhyne," Derrick said.

"Hi, Derrick. How many times do I have to ask you to call me Kate?"

"At least once more, Mrs. Rhyne," he said with a smile.

Kate laughed and headed to the kitchen. "A real gentleman. You'd better hang on to this one. He's rarer than rare."

"Hey, you," Derrick said as he stepped into the house and leaned down to kiss Cassie's forehead.

"Hey, you, back. "At least once more, Mrs. Rhyne?' What was that?" Cassie laughed.

"*Pirates of the Caribbean*."

"No kidding," she chortled. "I don't even think she got it."

Derrick shook his head with a grin.

"So, anyway, where've you been? You were supposed to help me with the stalls today, in case you forgot." Cassie tried to sound stern, but her excitement at seeing him made her words sound more like a pout, and she resented her weakness.

"Yeah, about that. Sorry. I sort of had it out with my mother this morning."

"Again? God, Derrick, you really need to knock that junk off. Why do you fight with them so much?"

Derrick frowned and moved away.

Cassie pulled on his arm. "Hey, I'm sorry. I didn't mean to blame you. So, what happened?"

His eyes grayed and he stared out the large bay window at the horses galloping in the pasture. A slow smile crossed his lips. "Nothing much. It was stupid. Not worth talking about." He pulled her by the hand and wrapped his arms around her. "What's up for the rest of the day?"

"We were just getting ready to eat breakfast. I'm positive Clara made more than enough. Come on."

"What about the stalls?"

"Duh, they're done," she grinned. "Well, most of them, anyway. I figured we could do the rest after we ride. The horses will be done eating by then, and Noah should have them all outside. I think you can use Dillon again if you want."

Derrick laughed. "Noah? That old fart? I don't know why your mother keeps him on."

"Because she's as loyal to him as he is to her. He's been with our family for, like, forty years. He wouldn't know what to do with himself if she let him go. He'd probably shrivel up and die."

"I'm surprised he's not already dead. He's got to be, what, ninety?"

Cassie giggled. "No! He's not ninety. He's more like sixty-something. And he's in pretty good shape, for an old man."

"Doesn't he have sons to help out?"

"He does, but my mom doesn't care for them much. She told them she'd prefer if they didn't come around the property unless it was very important. The older one, George, has been after my mom since before my dad died. She says he turns her stomach. He turns mine, too."

Derrick chuckled. "That sucks. What about the other one?"

"Hank. He's okay. Sort of a follower of George. He seems sweet enough but does everything his brother tells him to, good or bad."

Derrick grinned. "Oh, a kiss ass."

"Not nice."

"Hey," he said and wrapped his arms around her waist. "How about I finish up the lower barn stalls while you ride, and then let me take you out for a drive when you're through?"

"Why? You finally going to tell me that deep, dark secret you've been hiding from me?" she teased.

Derrick's expression darkened, but he quickly shifted gears with a shrug. "Nah, but I do have a surprise for you. Not a big surprise, something small, but I think you'll like it."

"Oh, really? I love surprises. And I get the better end of the stick all the way around. I get to ride *and* I get out of mucking the rest of the stalls. Awesome!"

Kate called from the kitchen. "Cassie, you kids eating?"

Cassie rolled her eyes. "Yeah, we're coming."

###

Derrick and Cassie walked out to the porch and Cassie stretched her arms toward the pale blue sky. "I'm stuffed," she said and patted at the perspiration on her neck.

"Clara's a great cook. I'm surprised you don't all weigh three hundred pounds."

Cassie chuckled. "They're trying to get me there. Mom thinks I need fattening up."

"Yeah, well, I think you're pretty perfect just the way you are."

"Yeah? You think I rock the shorts and work boots look? Sexy or what?"

"Mmm, sexy. Definitely sexy."

He nuzzled her neck and Cassie's legs weakened. Desire raged within and her palms broke into instant sweat. She broke from his grasp and faced him, standing up on her toes to whisper in his ear. "I want you."

"What, here? Now?" he spat out the words.

She laughed at his excitement. "How's it feel?"

"Like torture," he moaned. "That wasn't nice."

"Well, if it's any consolation, I do want you."

Derrick pulled her into him again and pressed his hardness against her. Cassie moaned.

"Where can we go?" he whispered.

She pulled away reluctantly and calmed her breathing. "Unfortunately, there's no place around here."

Derrick straightened up. "Soon then." He smiled and glanced past Cassie to the north field. "Is that Arco out there?"

"Yeah."

"Come on, I'll help you catch him."

"I don't need help catching him. He'll come when I call him.

Watch." She skipped down to the golf cart and took two carrots from under the seat, then headed to the gate. "Wait here," she said as she climbed through the bars.

Arco grazed under the weeping willow by the brook. Cassie whistled and lifted the black leather halter and lead line from the rail. Arco's head shot up. He whinnied and broke into a gallop in Cassie's direction. The image of the large jet black animal shining under the morning sun and the sound of thunderous hoof beats only yards away would be enough to unnerve almost anyone, but not Cassie. She knew Arco, and trusted him. She laughed and stretched out her arms, exposing the carrots in both hands.

As he closed the gap between him and Cassie, Derrick called out behind her. "Um, hey Cass, I think you should back up to the fence."

Arco skidded to a halt just feet in front of her and shook his head, sending his long wavy mane and forelock sailing in the wind. Cassie smiled. "You're gorgeous, and you know it. What a show off." She held up one of the carrots and let him bite off half. "Hey, big man, I feel like riding the wind. You up for it?" She laughed and patted his neck, and then slid the halter over his head. She slid the clip of the lead line through the ring on the left then slipped it through the end of the lead line to make a slipknot.

"Where's his bridle?" Derrick asked.

"Don't need one. I'm only going to hack." She flung the lead line over to the other side and clipped it on the other ring. Grabbing a handful of mane, she flung herself up on his back. "I'm all yours," she said and wrapped her legs tight around his drum.

"So, you're good then?"

"Better than good. This is my favorite type of riding."

"I'm outta here, then. I have stalls to muck out. See you in about an hour."

"Okay. Tk tk, come on, boy," she said, and squeezed Arco forward. It didn't take much to get him galloping off.

Cassie threw her hands out to her sides and tipped her face to the sky with her eyes closed. Tail and hair danced in the wind in unison.

She straightened up and grabbed hold of the makeshift reins and guided Arco toward a large fallen tree trunk near the left of the field, then leaned forward and grasped him with her knees, laughing and coaxing him onward. They flew through the air and Cassie's stomach fluttered at the momentary loss of gravity. "That is so awesome!" she called to Arco.

They reached the brook and Cassie slid from Arco's back. She kicked off her work boots and socks and waded in the water. "Come on, you love it too. Here, you want the rest of your carrots? You have to come in and get them."

Arco started to the brook then raised his head with pricked ears and looked back toward the house.

In the far distance Cassie heard a small voice. "Cassie! Hey, Cassie!"

Cassie climbed out of the brook and pressed the water from her shorts, staring at the girl in the baseball cap approaching from the gate. "I wonder who that is."

Arco snickered then dropped his head to graze.

The girl slowed as she got closer to them. "Wow, this was further than I thought," she said, bending forward. She lowered her hands to her knees and breathed heavily. She stood upright and pulled her cap from her head. Long blond hair cascaded down her shoulders. "Hey, that looked great. What a jump! I want to try it."

Cassie's heart stood still. "What are you doing here?"

Belle pranced up to her and patted Arco on the back. "I came to ride, silly." She cast a glance back to where she came from and waved.

Cassie squinted in the same direction and saw Derrick standing at the gate. He didn't wave back. "I didn't know you were coming out this morning."

"I wasn't supposed to, but my father had something to talk with your mother about and he invited me along." Belle continued to stroke Arco's back. "He's a beauty. And so strong. He took that jump with no effort at all. Can I ride him?"

"Absolutely not. I told you—"

Belle shoved Cassie back and she tripped to the ground. In one swift motion, Belle grabbed a chunk of mane and tossed herself onto Arco's back. By the time Cassie got to her feet, Belle and Arco were galloping toward the downed tree.

"Belle! Stop him. You can't ride him without a saddle. You don't even have a helmet. Stop! You're going to hurt him!" Cassie raced after them. Time slowed and all movement followed. Arco and Belle raced through the middle of the field at full speed. Belle clung to his back the best she could, but her legs didn't seem to be able to hold her steady. She looked like an inexperienced rider the way she tossed around on his back.

Cassie ran toward the gate where Derrick stood and yelled, "Call my mother!"

Belle screamed and pulled on the makeshift reins, but without a bridle, nothing seemed to slow him down. "Cassie, stop him! Cassie!"

Arco veered and headed in Cassie's direction.

"Jump off!" Cassie yelled.

"Are you crazy? Stop him! Oh my God, he's going to try to jump the gate!"

Just before the gate, Cassie spun around, waved her arms, and yelled for Arco to stop. He continued to race forward and then suddenly sat back on his haunches and slid to a stop like a rodeo pony.

Belle screamed as she flew through the air and landed on the ground with a heavy thud.

CHAPTER SEVEN

Belinda rolled to her hands and knees and gasped for air. It took what seemed like an eternity for her wind to come back. She lifted her head enough to see her father and Kate rush from the porch, followed by Derrick. He ran past them, climbed through the bars of the gate, and grabbed Arco's halter.

"What the hell were you doing?" Derrick yelled back to her.

Belinda stood and limped her way toward the gate.

Cassie glared. "You're such an idiot. I told you he'd never let you ride him."

"That animal should be made into glue," Belinda shot back. "And by the way, yeah, I'm okay."

"Actually, I'm more concerned about my horse."

Belinda spun around to retaliate, but Cassie was already in stride with Derrick and Arco heading out of the pasture. "Little witch," Belinda mumbled. She winced and pressed her hand against her right thigh, then hobbled toward the gate where Mrs. Rhyne and her father stood waiting.

"Are you all right, dear?" asked Kate.

"Yes, no thanks to that beast. Like I told Cassandra, he should be made into glue."

Frank chuckled. "Now, come on, Belle, no need of that." He gazed past her toward Cassie and Arco, and then regarded Kate. "He looks like a fine animal. Yes, indeed, a fine animal."

Belinda caught the exchange and noticed Mrs. Rhyne shift with unease and a smile curved her lips. As usual, there was more going on here than her father's concern for her well-being.

Frank opened the gate and guided Belinda out. "Come on, Belle, I think we've overstayed our welcome for today."

"We should sue them, Father," Belinda said.

Again Kate flinched and Belinda grinned.

Frank laughed outright and draped his arm around Belinda's shoulders. "Now you sound like me." He glanced back at Kate. "But we don't sue friends, Babydoll."

Kate latched the gate and followed behind them. "No, you just force them into deals they don't want to make."

Frank stopped in his tracks with raised eyebrows. "You saying you changed your mind?"

"No. My decision is firm. That's not to say you haven't worked your brawn on others in this town."

Frank continued to his truck. He helped Belinda into the back seat of the King Cab and then looked toward Kate. "You still have three days to give it some thought. I'll see you at Charlie's law office on Tuesday."

"I'll be there ready to sign papers on the original deal. Nothing more," Kate said.

Frank nodded and tipped his hat, then rounded the truck to the driver's side and drove off.

Belinda sat up and glanced over the seat at Kate's receding image and smiled. "So, you want to tell me what's going on with you and Mrs. Rhyne?"

Frank smirked in the rear view mirror. "Just business."

"What kind of business can you do with people like that?"

"Land, honey. They have a lot of it and I want it," Frank said. "Now don't go flappin' your jaws about it, either. And I think it would be wise if you stopped bullying the daughter."

Belinda flashed him a surprised glare. "Bullying? I take offense to that. I'm not a bully. Everyone likes me."

"Yeah, everyone that you don't bully."

"Well, if I'm a bully, it's your fault," she said.

Frank glanced at her through the mirror with narrowed eyes, but didn't speak.

"Oh, come on, Daddy," she said in a sarcastic voice. "You know you're my hero. I want to be just like you when I grow up."

"You will be, don't you worry about that," he murmured.

Belinda stared out the side window at the trees speeding by. "Yeah, I know," she mumbled.

"What was that?" he asked.

"Why don't we ever talk? I mean really talk."

"We do talk. I don't know what you mean."

"Yeah, we talk business. It's always business. I mean talk about me, about school, about what I'm doing or who I'm dating. Talk to me the way Mrs. Rhyne talks to Cassandra."

He gave a quick glance to the mirror with furrowed eyebrows. "What do you mean, who you're dating? You're too young to date."

"I'm not. I'm sixteen and most girls in my school have been dating since they were twelve."

"Then most girls in that school are nothing more than tramps. Your mother and I have raised you better than that. You'll date when I say you date, and I better not find out about you doing it before."

Belinda set her gaze on the trees once again. His tone said the conversation was over, but Belinda knew otherwise. Her thoughts roamed to the most handsome boy she knew—Derrick Anderson. All the girls wanted him, but he avoided them completely. That is, except for Cassie.

A grin spread across her face. *But all the girls aren't me, and that includes you, Cassandra Rhyne. Derrick will be mine, you wait and see. Because I choose him to be. I choose you, Derrick, to be my first boyfriend, my first kiss...my first everything.*

CHAPTER EIGHT

Derrick sat upright in bed and glanced at the clock. The large green florescent numbers read 5:32. He smiled and got out of bed. Cassie would have nothing to scold him about this time.

He cleaned up and went downstairs, pulled two banana nut muffins from the tray near the microwave, and then slipped out of the house, avoiding yet another confrontation with his parents.

He arrived at Rhyne Farms at 6:15, the break of dawn. He took the right into the property and drove the long, dusty road to the red barn, careful to turn off his headlights so as not to disturb anyone. His thoughts drifted to the surprise he had planned for Cassie yesterday. Belle's little escapade may have delayed it a day, but today was a new day. He twirled his senior ring around his finger. Not quite an engagement ring, but the next best thing, in his opinion.

He crept the truck along the graveled drive and pulled up between the house and the red barn, and then glanced in his rear view mirror. "No freakin' way." Derrick got out and flashed a bright white dimpled smile at Cassie. "Mornin'."

"Where have you been? You should have been here five minutes ago," Cassie said.

Derrick furrowed his eyebrows. "Man, you're tough."

"If it were up to me, I'd dock you an hour. Noah's off and I was really counting on you to help," she said, and turned away from him.

Derrick followed behind. "Hey, I'm sorry. Really. I thought I was doing great, and—"

She faced him with a giggle. "Oh stop. I'm just teasing. Come on, really? Five minutes? I'm not a jerk, you know."

"I know," he said with a grin. "I was just playing along."

Cassie blushed and spun away. "Good. I've already finished feeding in the red barn. We just need to bring them in from the west field. After that, we can go up to the main barn and feed. You ready to help?"

"Sure."

"You remember where they all go, right?"

"Pretty sure. Any questions I'll be sure to ask you, Boss."

Cassie smiled over her shoulder. "Hmm, I think I like the sound of that."

Derrick laughed and headed to the west field.

"Hey, remember to be careful with King's Grant," she called after him. "Bring him in alone, not two-by-two. He doesn't play well when others are close."

"I remember," he yelled back and waved without turning.

Over the next few hours, they fed horses, brought them in, put them out, and mucked stalls.

Derrick studied Cassie every chance he got. He couldn't help it. There were so many things about her that he couldn't put into words. Like how she made him smile when he really didn't want to, or how a look from her would tickle his stomach and make him feel all weird. She gave his life stability, a meaning. Today. He would give her his ring today, before she left for her aunt's. His thoughts drifted to the first time he'd known he was hooked on her...

###

Two months earlier

It was April when they'd met. A new year, and a new beginning for Derrick and his family. They'd moved to Oaklandale for a fresh start after...

Derrick shook his head away from the dark and pulled his thoughts back to Cassie. He'd been searching for a reason to live ever since *that day*. Now, as he sat in the back of senior English class, tilting his chair on two of its legs staring at the girl in the second row, the second seat from the door, he believed he'd found that reason. She was the only girl who hadn't thrown herself at him, and ironically she was the only girl he wanted to talk to. So much so, that he took a part time job on her farm just to get the chance. She was kind, gentle, and helpful - she'd given him the answers to the history homework- - and she had the sweetest smile he'd ever remembered seeing.

Cassie had leaned over to talk to the girl sitting next to her and Derrick saw her glance back in his direction. She sent him one of those smiles that reaches in and takes your words away. Embarrassed at being caught staring, all he could manage was a faint smile back.

The bell rang and Cassie gathered her things to leave. Derrick rushed up behind her. "Hey, what do you have next?"

Cassie turned, startled. "Oh, hey. I'm free next period. I have Study Hall so I'm heading home early."

Derrick followed her into the hallway. "Lucky you. I'm thinking of bailing from Psych, but…"

Cassie tipped her head to the side and smirked. "Not a good idea. If my mother found out she'd fire you for sure."

"Yeah, and this being my second day on the job, that would suck. Besides, I sort of like being around you," he said with his best attempt at flirting.

Most girls would have swooned, but not Cassie. She simply smiled and kept walking.

"What about you?" he asked.

"What about me?"

He moved in front of her and continued walking backwards. "Do you like being around me?"

Cassie laughed. "Yeah, you're okay."

Derrick held his hand to his heart. "Okay? Is that all? Your arrow strikes straight and true."

Again Cassie laughed out loud. She stopped and glanced at the staring girls. "Look around, Derrick. I'm the one being shot with arrows, and they're tipped with jealous poison. If you keep flirting with me, you're sure to get me killed."

"Ah, but at least you noticed I was flirting. That's a start at least."

Cassie blushed and Derrick's heart raced. He loved her innocence.

"Are you working at the barn today?" Cassie asked.

"Of course. I'm working every day."

"Why did you volunteer for every day? Don't you want to play sports or something?"

Derrick moved up beside her and became serious. "Yeah, I suppose, but not this year. I want to take some time to focus. You know, getting acclimated to a new school, new friends, new home, and now a new job; that sort of stuff takes a lot out of you. Besides, working at your barn provides three great benefits."

"Such as?" Cassie asked and tilted her head with a grin.

He raised three fingers, ticking off his list as he spoke. "Well, it keeps me out of trouble, puts me around horses—which I like—and lets me see you every day."

Again Cassie blushed. "Okay, well, I'll see you later then."

Derrick watched her until she was at the student parking lot, when an arm landed across his back and pushed him forward.

"Dude! What are you doing? That girl doesn't date. I mean anyone. You're wasting your time," David Campton said. "Anyway," he continued with a shrug, "we're heading over to Lloyd's for some basketball after Psych. You game?"

"Nah, can't. I have to work."

"Oh, yeah. I can't believe you went as far as taking a job at her farm. Dude, you got it bad."

Derrick pushed David's shoulder. "Get out of here. You don't know what you're talking about. I needed a job and thought working outdoors with animals for a decent wage beat the hell out of the mall."

"Yeah, maybe. But I think that's only part of it," David said.

They went to their lockers—which were only three apart from each other—and exchanged their English books for their Psych books.

"Hey," David said, "Lloyd's folks are going out of town for the Fourth and he's throwing a bangin' party. Has he asked you yet?"

Derrick's stomach tightened. "No."

"Well, consider yourself asked. And you better be there," David said and punched him in the arm.

"Don't think I'm going to be able to do that."

David stopped in the hall as if he'd been hit square in the stomach. "What do you mean? You have to. It's not an option."

Derrick slammed his locker shut then walked down the hallway. David followed close behind.

"Care to 'splain?" David asked.

"Not really. I'm not going, that's all."

David moved up in front of Derrick and stopped him with a hand to his chest. "Hey, man, I've been your best friend since you got here."

"That's not a title you should be proud of," Derrick said.

"Whatever. Fact remains. So spill it."

Derrick sighed and tried to walk around him, but David stood solid. He looked around. Most of the kids had already cleared the halls for class. "All right, the short and sweet of it is I moved here to get away from trouble. Start fresh. I don't do parties, or as you may have noticed, hang with many people. Life's simpler that way."

"Just stop by for a drink, then."

"I don't drink," Derrick said and moved around David who didn't stop him this time.

"Now that's just wrong. What do you mean you don't drink? All teenage individuals with any sense of self-respect drink."

Derrick rolled his eyes. "That's exactly why I don't drink, you idiot, because I have self-respect. Besides, it's not as cool as everyone makes it out to be. If you had half a brain, you wouldn't drink either."

"I happen to enjoy it," David said.

"Then I repeat, you're an idiot."

"And you're a jerk, but I still love ya," David said with a grin.

"Whatever. Hey, you think Cassie's going?"

"Are you kidding? She doesn't go to those things. Too high and mighty for that."

Derrick frowned and moved ahead.

"Nah, what I mean is we invite her but she always 'respectfully declines,'" David said with an upper-class drawl. "She doesn't even date, man. That's why you're wasting your time."

"I wonder why. She's definitely pretty enough."

David flipped off a kid who came around the corner too fast and just about mowed him down, then moved his attention back to Derrick. "Something about a guy she dated a year ago. Turned out pretty ugly, I guess. The guy didn't get what he wanted, but decided to spread rumors around school that said he did. Put Cassie through hell, from what I remember. She hasn't dated since." He punched Derrick's shoulder. "Not that guys haven't tried, though."

The warning bell rang and they walked in silence to psych class. David stopped him before entering the classroom. "Hey man, something happened before you moved here. Tell me what it was."

Derrick closed his eyes briefly and shook his head. When he opened them, he stared intensely at David then moved closer, his eyes burning from memory, "I—"

Mr. Hatch flung open the door. "What are you boys doing out

here? Didn't you hear the bell? Get in here and take your seats."

Derrick, still staring into David's eyes, grinned. "Another time, buddy."

###

The whinny of a horse brought Derrick back to the present. He poured the last bucket of grain into Sampson's feed bin and wiped the sweat from his forehead. The clock by the feed room read eleven o'clock. Break time.

Derrick climbed the steps to the second floor observatory and pulled an apple from the fruit bowl on the coffee table in front of the long plexi-glass window. He was just about to put his coins in the vending machine for an O.J. when he heard the door open behind him. He glanced back and smiled. "Hey, fancy meeting you here." He put in more change in the machine and pressed the label for a Coke. The can dropped and he handed it to Cassie.

Cassie smiled back. "Guess great minds think alike."

"Hey, I meant to tell you. There's one horse left out in the north pasture. I couldn't catch him. Big ass beast, lots of muscles. He gave me a stare down and he won. I don't remember him. Is he new?"

Cassie scowled. "Yeah, and you'd never guess whose horse it is. His name is Goliath."

Derrick grinned. "Belinda's."

"Good guess. He came in last night. We tried to put him in a stall, but he kicked the hell out of it. Mom was afraid he was going to hurt himself, so she told me to put him out in the north pasture. We're going to have to get him in before Queen of the Damned shows up, or I'm sure she'll raise hell's army."

"Maybe we can do it together. Two against one should put the odds in our favor."

Cassie nodded with a smile. She took a long drink of soda and then belched. "Oops, sorry," she giggled. "Oh, hey, are you still able to take care of the horses on Wednesday?"

"Wednesday? Oh, yeah, Fourth of July. Sure, no problem."

"Awesome. That's going to make my mom really happy. We haven't seen my aunt in like, forever." She finished her drink and threw the can away. "Okay, ready?" she asked and started down the stairs.

Derrick pointed to the golf cart parked in the midway to the barn. Teddy, the rusty Appaloosa, stood on the cross-ties in front of it. "Go get the cart and meet me at the feed room. I'll unhook Teddy and put him in his stall."

Cassie pulled up with the cart and Derrick dumped two bales into the small trailer hooked to the back. He gave a nod over his shoulder. "Looks like we have company."

Cassie looked out of the barn toward the house on the hill and saw two girls walking briskly toward the main barn.

"Oh, great. The wicked witch has arrived and she brought her little dog, too. That's all I need."

Derrick put Teddy in his stall, unhooked the lead line, and patted him before leaving and sliding the door shut. "Two peas in a pod, my mom would say."

"Yeah, you got that right," Cassie said with a pout.

"Weren't you and Jess friends for a while?"

"Yeah, but when I say she was trouble, I'm not kidding. She

screwed me over more than once. You might think with a father as the sheriff she'd do whatever to stay out of trouble, but not her. Seemed the more she could do to get under her father's skin, the better it made her feel. He was getting ready to land us both in juvenile detention. My mother gave me an ultimatum: give up Jess or give up Arco."

Derrick put his arm around her shoulders. "You made the right choice."

Cassie took her pocket knife from her pants pocket and cut the hay rope. She yanked two flakes off and tossed them in Jasmine's stall. Teddy snickered in anticipation. "Yeah, I guess. And then Belle nearly getting herself killed by hijacking Arco from me yesterday. That so pissed me off. She really could have hurt him." She pulled two more flakes and threw them in the next stall. Again, Teddy snickered.

###

Cassie watched helplessly as Belinda strode into the barn with an upturned nose. She wished there was a door she could have slammed in her face.

Belle leaned toward Jess. "We've just come from the lower barn where they keep the hags." She chuckled. "Oh, sorry. I mean the barn horses." She lowered her voice. "They use them for lessons for people who don't have one of their own. Anyway, this is the big barn where Goliath will be when he gets back from training.

"Hi, Cassie," Jessica Winslow said with an uncomfortable smile.

Cassie paused and then nodded. Too much had passed between Jess and Cassie for her to forgive.

Belinda scowled at Jess. "Are you nuts? Why in the world would you talk with the help? They work for us."

"Get real, Belle," Jess said. She rolled her eyes and then gave a hoity-toity shake of the head.

Cassie snickered. "Anyway, Belinda, what do you want?"

"I came to ride. I understand my horse came in last night. Go and tack him up for me."

Cassie pulled two more flakes off the bale and walked in front of Belinda. She fluffed them up, dropping pieces of straw over her boots. Belinda peered down and opened her mouth to complain, but hay dust climbed up her nose and she sneezed instead.

Cassie smirked. "I'm feeding, in case you didn't notice. And I'm not here as your servant. That beast of yours wouldn't take to a stall so he spent the night outside in the north pasture. You can catch him and tack him yourself."

"We'll see about that," Belinda said. She eyed Derrick with a provocative grin. "How about you? You want to tack *me* up?" She moved closer to him and played her finger down the side of his face.

Derrick pulled away. "Knock it off, Belle."

She eyed him up and down slowly, taking in his cowboy boots, dark blue jeans, and navy T-shirt that fit tight around his athletic body. "Mm-mmm, I'd pay you double just to watch you work," Belle said and winked.

"You must be joking," he said, yanking his gloves on tighter. He shook his head with a sarcastic laugh and then headed out of the barn. As he walked past Cassie, he stopped, lowered his lips to hers, and gave her a long, sensuous kiss. "I'm going to get the other horses."

Cassie's heart raced and for the briefest of moments, she forgot anyone else was there. His voice alone caused ripples in her blood. Her gaze followed him down the long hallway to the end of the aisle. The brightness from outside cast his image in shadow.

"Hot guy in aisle three," Jess joked.

Belinda shot daggers at her through tightly narrowed eyes. Cassie half expected to see steam seep from her ears and the image made her laugh out loud.

Belinda stomped past her. "Yeah, get a good laugh now, witch. We'll see who wins this game." She stormed out of the barn. "Jess, what the hell? Are you coming or what?"

"Don't let her worry you," Jess said to Cassie. "She's just used to getting everything she wants, but she's all talk, really."

"Trust me, she doesn't scare me. Why do you even hang with her, Jess? You used to make fun of people like her."

Jess shrugged. "It's not like I have a lot of friend options, right?"

Cassie turned away from Jess's hard stared and grabbed a push broom. "No, I guess you don't."

"That's what I thought," Jess mumbled and then followed Belinda.

###

Belinda yanked hard on Jess's arm as they walked toward the north pasture. "Listen, I want dirt on Derrick."

"What can I do? It's not like he's going to open up to me knowing I'm friends with you."

"Your father's the bloody sheriff. I'm sure you can get something." Belinda's face burned with anger. "That little witch thinks she's a match for me? Hmpf. Who's she kidding? I'll tear her up and spit her out. By the time my father's done with her and her precious mother, she won't have anything left."

Jess chuckled. "For a minute I thought you said *you'd* tear her up and spit her out; now it's your father?"

"Same thing."

CHAPTER NINE

Cassie sat on the white fence and watched the sun as it peeked through the morning mist casting a ghost-like glow over the north pasture. Arco grazed in the distance in his favorite spot by the old weeping willow tree. She waited patiently—or so she thought—for Derrick to arrive to help with the morning chores of feeding and turning out as he'd promised. She glanced down at her watch for the umpteenth time, and toyed with her bottom lip. Every so often she'd glance over her shoulder at the long dirt road behind her. The air had already heated to a humid 75 degrees and would be in the 80's within the hour.

She tsked with annoyance and leaped from the fence. Part of her was frustrated that she allowed him to make her insides twist and turn, but another part of her reeled with a strange excitement. He was different. She knew deep within her heart that she could trust him. And he said he loved her. She felt her face flush with the thought and smiled.

Gravel crunched behind her in the distance and she spun toward the sound. The truck made its way up the long dirt road, melodically appearing between the tall live oak draped in Spanish moss that lined its path. She smiled and waved. Derrick beeped his horn in return.

Good grief, girl. Get some control.

Moments later, he parked his truck by the red barn.

"Well, happy Fourth of July. About time you showed up," Cassie called to him. "Just 'cause it's a holiday doesn't mean you can wander in whenever you feel like it. We have tons to get done before I leave."

Derrick jogged toward her, his muscled body swayed with the grace of a lion and Cassie found it difficult to take her eyes off of him. His intoxicating smile urged her to kiss him.

His lips were on hers before she could react to her own desire and for a moment that familiar heat of passion flowed between them. Cassie hated when it ended. She wanted him to hold her, kiss her…make love to her all day and all night. They hadn't done it yet, but she knew it would be soon. It had to be, or she'd die for sure. Headlines would read, "Girl's Body Heats Up and Burns to a Pile of Ash from the Heat of Passion."

So, this is what an addiction feels like.

The sound of the tractor out in the west field broke through their solitary world. They pulled apart, both shaking as they stared into each other's eyes.

"Noah's working today so we can finish up quicker," Cassie explained. She needed space to catch her breath. She moved away, leaned on the fence, and nodded toward Arco. "I swear that horse could eat this whole field in a day if I let him."

Derrick leaned on the fence beside Cassie and rested his cheek on his arm. "Beautiful," he said softly.

Cassie glanced at him and blushed. "Yes, he is, and he knows it."

"I wasn't talking about Arco."

How is it possible for one person to make you feel like this? She turned quickly and headed toward the red barn at a run. "Race you."

"I'll give you a head start," he called to her back. "You'll need it."

She continued to run at full speed without a glance back. She'd beat him in one game, at least. She approached the barn and prepared to slow when he breezed by her without a sound.

He stopped and leaned against the barn with a feigned yawn. "I need a coffee. I'm running a little slow this morning."

"Ha, ha, very funny," she said through heavy breaths. She punched him in the arm and then fell into him, laughing.

They performed the morning chores in a comfortable silence. It seemed as if every time Cassie glanced at him his eyes were on her and she warmed inside. *Please, God, don't let this be too good to be true.*

They broke three hours later and went to the snack room. "Want a soda?" Cassie asked as she reached in and grabbed a Coke.

"Sure, got any Mountain Dew?"

Cassie handed him his soda and sat on the counter by the sink. "My mom said to make sure I thanked you for taking care of the barn today and tomorrow."

"Not a problem. I'm happy to do it."

"Your parents don't mind? I mean, they don't mind you staying here in the guest house?"

"No," Derrick mumbled.

Cassie took a long, slow sip of her Coke and stared at him over the rim. "Your folks aren't doing anything for the Fourth?"

"Same thing they do every year, I suppose. Mom will grill some burgers and make a potato salad. They'll eat, have some sort of corny Fourth of July dessert, and then watch television. That's about it. We don't do fireworks or anything. I won't be missing much."

"Really? I love fireworks."

Derrick smiled. "Well, if you were staying around here, I'd be happy to do them with you."

Cassie giggled and slid slowly off the counter. "Mmm, I bet you'd do them with me," she said, leaning into his body.

Derrick wrapped both arms around her and pulled her to him. His hardness pressed against her groin and she moaned. Cassie felt his heart race beneath his T-shirt and she kissed his chest.

Still holding her by the waist, he leaned back and asked, "So what time are you leaving today to go to your aunt's?"

"Mom said we needed to be ready about two o'clock. Sorry, but I guess you'll be doing the afternoon feeding by yourself."

"Again, not a problem. I think I found my niche. This is my thing."

"Yeah? Me too. Its butt kicking, but I love it." Cassie gulped the rest of her soda, placed the can in the sink beside her, and glanced at her watch. "It's almost eleven. We have time to ride up to the brook for a quick dip, if you want."

"Yeah, sounds great to me."

Cassie made to leave the barn. "Dillon seemed a little lame when I pulled him in earlier. You should ride Sampson. He's in the fifth stall on the left; go ahead and pull him and start tacking. He wears the saddle on peg five in the tack room, and the bridles are all hung under the horses' names. Remember to leave his halter on under the bridle so we can let him graze. Pull Arco's tack for me, will you? I'm going to go get him. Be right back."

They tied the horses on the cross-ties in the aisle, brushed them out and tacked them up side by side. Cassie couldn't remember enjoying anyone's presence more.

Cassie led Arco out and mounted him. "I want to show you something first. We'll ride around the north pasture toward those woods. I've been out there and I think you'll like it. Very swampy and mysterious," she said.

Derrick led Sampson out behind Cassie. "Sure, I love the element of the mysterious. I'm with you, aren't I?" he said as he mounted.

"Very funny."

They led the horses at a walk past the lower barns, then broke into a slow trot toward the north pasture. A dust cloud from the dirt road caught Cassie's attention and she squinted to make out the approaching vehicle. "Whose this?" She looked at Derrick and saw his frown. She glanced back toward the car. "Oh, you're kidding me. What's Belinda doing here today?"

"Never mind. It doesn't matter. Let's just go for our ride. Maybe she'll be gone when we get back."

"Good idea." Cassie asked Arco for a slow canter. A few minutes later the pasture ended, replaced by large oak trees and still, marshy waters. Cassie dismounted and slid the reins over Arco's head. "Come on," she said, and tied Arco to a tree branch.

Derrick followed suit. Cassie took hold of Derrick's hand and led him a short distance into the marsh.

"Careful where you step," she said, pointing down. "Follow my footsteps exactly."

"Right." He followed a few more feet and then asked, "Hey, what about gators?"

Cassie giggled. "Yeah, they're here. But don't worry. They won't bother you unless you wade in the water, and we're not going to do that. That's why I want you to follow me exactly." She nodded to her left. "See? There's one over there. You have to look careful under the mist."

Derrick followed her gaze. "Oh man, that guy has his mouth open."

"He's hot."

"Yeah, well it's freaking me out. Why do they sit with their mouths open like that?"

"Two reasons, really. One, like I said, is to cool off. They don't have sweat glands so they leave their mouths open. They even pant like a dog, sometimes. The other reason is to let the plovers get rid of parasites."

"Plovers?"

Cassie pointed by the gator. "There, see those small birds?"

"Weird, I thought those birds stayed by the beaches."

"Apparently not. They've been around here as long as I can remember."

"Cool," Derrick said, but kept his eyes locked on the gator.

Cassie giggled and pulled him along. "He's not the only one in here, you know."

"Trying to make me feel better? How sweet."

"I just want to bring you in a little deeper, where it gets a bit darker. It's my favorite part of the marsh." She dropped his hand in order to navigate better.

Derrick rounded out to Cassie's left and came up beside her. Cassie stared wide-eyed. "Derrick, what are you doing? Get back behind me like I told you."

Derrick stopped, startled, and looked around quickly. "What? What's wrong? You see one of those things?"

"No, there's nothing near you. It's just that there's a lot of quicksand in here. You have to be very careful."

"Quicksand?! Really, Cass? I'm beginning to wonder if you're some psycho chick, luring me out here so I can get eaten by a gator and then chuck what's left of me into some quicksand."

"Oh, come on," Cassie said, and laughed out loud. "Hmm, that would be a thought for someone else I can think of though, now that you mention it."

Derrick moved in stride behind Cassie. "That's not nice, Cass."

Cassie smirked and glanced away. "Lighten up. It's not like I would do it."

They walked a few more yards before Cassie looked back at Derrick. "So, what do you think?"

The temperature dropped about ten degrees and the air filled with moisture. A soft mist fell across the bed of the marsh, and a slow breeze swayed the long strands of moss from the trees and stirred the mist.

"I love it. Eerie, yet beautiful. Just like you said, mysterious."

Cassie stared straight ahead and smiled. "Yeah, if you stay still and watch carefully, sometimes you can see the spirits of the marsh in the mist."

Derrick stared down at her and Cassie shifted her stance. "Can you hear the spirits now?" he asked.

"No. It's not like they talk to me all the time. But sometimes they warn me of things."

"Warn you? What do you mean? What kinds of warnings?"

Cassie set her eyes on his. "I know it sounds stupid, and you probably think I'm insane."

Eric's voice softened. "No, not at all. What do you mean they warn you? What do they sound like?"

Cassie turned away and stared off into the mist. "It's not actual words that I hear. It's more like a feeling. It's hard to explain. Sometimes I think that what I feel are the words they want me to hear. It started around the time Grandpa Joe died. I was sitting out here," Cassie pointed toward a large old Oak across the river, "over there under that tree, crying my eyes out. All of a sudden I heard this voice—or felt it—tell me to get up quickly. I don't know why, exactly, but I did. Good thing, too. There was a gator climbing up the bank not very far away from me. I was able to run back through those trees and get away from it."

"That's cool." Derrick reached for a branch and swung around the side of a tree. "I'm curious, though, that you would believe that there are spirits out here. I mean, I thought your family believed in God and all that."

"We do. What's that got to do with anything?"

"Nothing, I mean, well I thought that Bible thumpers didn't believe in ghosts."

Cassie snickered. "I never said we were Bible thumpers. Just because we believe in God doesn't mean we can't believe in spirits. I believe in both, actually. In fact, my Grandpa Joe used to say they were the lost souls with unfinished business and that as soon as they settle whatever it is that they need to settle, they would be able to go to wherever they are meant to go."

"So, how do you know they're good spirits? I mean, what if some of them are like poltergeists or something?"

"God, Derrick, you've watched too many movies."

"What? You can believe in ghosts—"

"Spirits," Cassie corrected.

"Okay, spirits, but you can't believe in poltergeists?"

"Whatever."

"Just sayin'."

Neither spoke for several minutes.

"What else do they say?"

"So you can make fun of me?"

"I'd never do that, Cassie, I'm really curious."

Cassie tilted her head. "You believe me?"

"I want to understand."

"But you don't believe me."

"I didn't say that."

Cassie shrugged. "Other stuff." She stared deep into Derrick's eyes. "Like, they told me my father was murdered."

"Cass, I…"

Cassie spun away. "It's nothing. My shrink says I make this crap up to cover my inner torment. She says I hear them say what my mind believes to be true, even if it isn't."

"You think she's right?"

Cassie shook her head slowly.

Derrick broke contact and moved away. "It must be great out here at night."

"I wouldn't know. I've never been out here at night. Now *that* would be suicide."

"Is this part of your land?" Eric said spreading his arms around him.

"This is all called Bayou Rhyne, but this part here is actually Miller property. It sort of intertwines with ours, though. If we had a canoe we could get to the property that my grandfather sold to Noah and his sons. They have a cabin about a mile in. That's one reason they wanted Old Man Miller's land when he died, because it would give them that much more of a continuation of land. That, and the fact that they were related and they felt they deserved his land anyway. Only he didn't have a will. As far as I understand, there was something about Noah's sons faking a will and Mr. Larson finding out about it. Now Larson has the land tied up in the courts. Seems he wants that property, too."

"But it's all marsh. Why would anyone want this? I mean, what's it good for?"

Cassie chuckled. "It's not all marsh. The Miller plantation pans out about a hundred acres, including marsh. The farm he had was well run and well set up. It would make great development land for anyone with the right funds." She bent down and picked up a stick covered in moss. When she stood, Derrick's eyes, wide with fright, made her freeze.

"What? What is it?"

"What the hell is that? It's huge!" he said and pointed behind her. "You nearly put your head in it."

Cassie followed his finger. A web spanned between two trees and held a large spider that reached about eight inches. Its long, thin, black and yellow legs and plump yellow and red two-inch oval body gave it a menacing appearance. Cassie shuddered. "Oh my God. I didn't even see that. I hate those things. Banana spiders freak me out."

"Yeah, me too apparently." Derrick shuddered. "So, why do you come in here if you know those things are here?s

Cassie smiled. "What am I supposed to do? Let them chase me away from the things I love? They're all over the barns, too, you know. Not just them either, other types too. Next time you're in the barn, take a look up." She smiled and moved into his arms. "Besides, why would I be afraid when I have my big, strong, male protector by my side?"

Derrick smiled down at her. "Yeah, that's right, and don't you forget it. And if that spider knew what was good for him, he'd pack it up and move out right about now." He leaned down and kissed her.

Cassie laid her head against his chest. "So, besides the spiders and the gators—oh yeah, and the snakes—what do you think of this place?"

Derrick laughed. "Honestly? I get why you love it here. It's definitely one of my favorites now, too."

They stayed a few minutes more, each in their own thoughts. Cassie smiled as she watched Derrick. She knew he'd love it here. She knew he'd understand.

A soft breeze stirred and Cassie tensed.

He isn't what he seems.

###

Derrick stared at Cassie as they sat by the brook in a small field on the other side of the woods and let the horses graze. Cassie threw a stone in the water and watched the swirls pan out and disappear. Her beauty consumed him and he wanted nothing more than to take her, right here, right now.

Instead, he rolled onto his side and rested his head on his hand. He cleared his throat. "So tell me about the Miller place. Why so much controversy? I hear a lot about it around town."

"Like I said, the Larsons are trying to buy it. It used to be a beautiful spread, but now it's all run down and some folks say it's haunted."

"Why haunted?"

"Old Man Miller was killed there about three years ago. Right after we moved in here, actually."

"Why would someone kill him?"

"The police say it looked like a robbery. But other people say he was murdered for his land."

Derrick sat up. "His land? And now Larson is interested in it?"

Cassie chuckled. "Wow, you're quick. Putting it all together, are you?"

Derrick found himself running out of arguments to defend Larson. Maybe Cassie was on to something. Maybe she…

Cassie continued. "He throws his weight around as if he already owns the town. God forbid if he makes mayor."

Derrick stood up. "Hey, take me out to the Miller farm. I want to check it out."

"No, I don't have time. And we especially don't want to go through that way," she said, pointing toward the woods on the other side of the brook. "There's tons of quicksand. There used to be a path between our property and his, but most of it has grown over. You'd really have to know your way around before trying to get through now. The horses would never make it."

Derrick sat down and laid back beside Cassie. "Hey Cass, I want to tell you something but I don't want you to freak out or anything."

Cassie rested on her elbow and glanced down at him. "Sure. You can tell me anything."

His heart ached for her words to be true, but he wasn't sure she was ready for *that* truth yet. Would she judge him? Would she be able to forgive him? How could she when his own parents hadn't forgiven him, or worse, he couldn't even forgive himself?

He cleared his throat a second time and reached into his pocket.

"Well, since our drive never happened because of Belle's little accident yesterday, I couldn't do what I had planned."

Cassie tilted her head and squinted down at him.

He leaned up on his elbow and held out a bunched up tissue. "I wanted to give you this."

She took the tissue and unfolded it.

He smiled at her deep intake of breath.

"No way." she whispered.

"Well? Are you going to take it?"

Cassie reached out her hand and spread her fingers. "The middle one, it's fatter."

Derrick slipped his senior ring on her finger and smiled. "I'm glad, Cass. Thanks for accepting it."

"Are you kidding? I love you, Derrick. This is perfect."

But then her expression clouded and his heart skipped a beat. "What's wrong?" he asked.

Cassie played with a piece of grass between her legs.

He rose to his feet and walked to the edge of the brook. He reached down and grabbed two small rocks and tossed them in the water. A soft touch prickled his skin and he looked down to see Cassie gazing up at him.

"Derrick, I'm sorry."

He swam mightily against the currents in her beautiful blue eyes, but found himself drowning in them nonetheless. "Why?" he murmured. "You change your mind already?"

She looked down at her feet. "No, of course not. It's just…I don't know. You make me feel all…I don't know…twisted inside."

"Yeah, you make me feel the same way. But that's a good thing, right?"

Cassie rendered a small smile.

"Listen, Cass, I know it's scary. It scares me, too. I wasn't looking for a girlfriend, Lord knows that. But here you are."

"Derrick, I—"

"I think we could be good together. We have a lot in common, don't you think?"

"Yes. I don't know, I guess I'm just afraid of being hurt. I couldn't take it if you hurt me."

Derrick's heart tightened. "Cass, how do you feel about the past?"

"What do you mean?"

"I mean, things that have happened in the past."

Cassie rested her hand on his chest. "I know you have secrets, Derrick."

"You do?"

"The spirits have been trying to tell me for weeks."

Derrick took her hands. "It doesn't matter. Whatever happened in the past is just that, the past, right? We leave it there and move on…together. Can you do that? Can you forgive the past and move on with me, Cassie?"

"Yeah, I think so." She gazed up at him, her head tilted to the side. "But, when are you going to unlock your secrets, Derrick?"

Derrick cleared his throat and looked toward the brook. She wasn't ready for this. He wasn't ready for this. "When I can face the demons that hold the key."

His mouth dried. Year-old images raced through his mind as vivid as if it were yesterday.

And then the scream. *Oh my God, turn!*

The next thing he remembered was waking up on the ground…and Danny's bloodied body beside him.

Cassie stood and brushed the dirt off her butt. "I gotta get going. Mom wants to be ready to leave by 3:00 today."

Derrick shook his head to scatter the ghosts back to the past. "Thanks. Hey, tell your mom no worries about the barn. I got this covered."

Cassie smiled. "Of course you do. We're not worried. She trusts you, and so do I."

CHAPTER TEN

Present Day

Derrick opened his eyes, dazed and confused. His truck faced the road from the edge of the woods at an awkward angle. A moment passed before reality set in. He jumped from his truck and looked through the rain with wild panic. A large mound lay struggling on the side of the road. Arco. He ran to him and strained to hear Belinda's voice.

Jess drove up beside the truck and screeched to a halt. She rushed to the front of her car and screamed. "Oh my God! Belle!"

"I can't find her!"

Jess reached in her back seat and pulled out a flashlight, and then ran to Derrick. "Belle, can you hear me? Belle!" she called as she shone the light into the woods.

"There! I see something," Derrick said, pointing to the ditch by the side of the road.

"Oh my God. This isn't real," Jess said.

Derrick got to his feet and faced Jess. Shock glazed her eyes. He grabbed her arm and shook her. "Call 911." She didn't move. He yanked on her arm again. "Jess!" She shook her head in slow motion. "I need you to call 911. I'm going to see if I can help her. *Now*, Jess."

She ran to the passenger side of her car, grabbed her purse and poured the contents on the road, and then rummaged for her cell phone. Satisfied, Derrick ran to Belinda. A moment later, Jess was by his side.

"What are we going to do?" she said through desperate tears.

"Did you call?"

"Yes, they're on their way."

"Then we wait for them."

"Derrick, she isn't moving. Is she dead?"

"No, she isn't dead! She has a pulse. I checked," Derrick snapped.

Jess shown the light on Belle's face. "She's *bleeding*."

Derrick stared in disbelief as blood spilled from a large gash in her head. He pulled off his shirt and pressed it against the wound.

"Derrick, there's so much blood." Jess kneeled beside him. "Belle, honey can you hear me? Belle, answer me. You're going to be okay. You hear me? You're going to be okay."

"She's unconscious. All we can do is wait."

Moments later, Deputy Richard Wheeler skidded to a stop behind Jess's vehicle.

Derrick's stomach lurched at the blur of commotion that followed. He stood and backed away from the gruesome sights in front of him. His head whirled. *Not again.*

"Son, you have to come with me. You're bleeding," someone said from his left.

"I'm fine," he told them. "Just take care of Belle."

Fire rescue, cruisers, and an ambulance littered the scene. Arco caught in Derrick's left peripheral vision and his eyes slowly drifted to the struggling animal. He watched as animal control shot him up with something. He watched as men hovered over Belle as they laid her on the gurney and rushed her toward the ambulance. He watched as Arco struggled to his feet and was led to the trailer.

He watched.

Because that's all the boulder in the pit of his stomach would allow him to do.

Somewhere in the back of his head he was speaking, answering questions that drifted into his conscious like waves on a rocky shore.

Someone placed a blanket around Derrick's shoulders and led him to the back of Deputy Wheeler's cruiser where Wheeler stood with his hands on his hips staring at the ambulance as it pulled away. He turned and slowly walked up to Derrick. "Ready for some more questions?"

Derrick nodded toward Jess who was sitting on the bumper of a fire truck being tended to by an EMT. "Is she okay?"

"About as good as can be expected after seeing her best friend's head bashed in."

Derrick's gaze bore into the deputy.

Wheeler smirked. "Want to tell me what happened here?"

"I already did."

"Yeah, I guess you did." The deputy strode to the trunk of his car and pulled out an instrument, and then walked to Derrick and gestured for him to move to the back of the vehicle. "This here is called a Breathalyzer. Ever take one before?"

"No," Derrick said and leaned against the car adjusting the blanket around his shoulders.

Wheeler raised his eyebrows. "Really? Now, see? There you have it. I would have figured you'd be a pro at this."

"I wasn't drinking."

"Well, you sure smell like you've been drinking. And Jess, over there, seems to think you were drinking."

Derrick's gaze shot over to Jess. "Is that what she said? She said I was drinking? She's lying!" he yelled, and Jess glance his way. "You lied! Why?" Jess looked away.

"You going to take this test for me?" Deputy Wheeler asked.

Derrick pushed off from the car. "Yeah, I'll take your stupid test because I wasn't drinking! Belle's the one who was drunk." He nodded toward Jess. "You going to make her take one, too?"

"This is just procedure, son. Nothing more."

"Yeah, and you're a liar! I want my father."

"After the test. I'll bring you in and you can call your parents."

###

Derrick sat in the back of the cruiser with his hands cuffed behind his back. "This is *bull*. I haven't been drinking, and you know it. The test is false."

Deputy Wheeler didn't respond.

"Is Belle all right?" No answer from the front. "I just want to know if she's going to be okay. Please!" Still no answer.

They arrived at the Oaklandale County Sheriff's Department fifteen minutes later. Wheeler walked him to an interrogation room and sat him at the small metal table in the middle of the room. A few moments passed, but to Derrick, it was more like hours. The door opened and a large-framed, balding, middle-aged man walked in.

"Sheriff, I'm glad you're here. Is Belle going to be okay? I asked Deputy Wheeler, but he won't talk to me."

"You just sit right there," Sheriff Sam Winslow said in a slow drawl. "And keep your mouth shut until I tell you to speak."

Derrick sat at the edge of his chair, his hands cuffed behind his back, and stared up at the man. "I haven't been drinking. I told you, Belinda threw—"

Winslow leaned his large, broad frame over the table and slammed his fists down. "You don't listen too well, do ya, boy?" He spoke slow and deliberate only inches from Derrick's face.

"I want to see my parents," Derrick stammered.

"When I say you do," Winslow said, and leaned even closer. "Because of your drunken ass, there's a young girl laying in a coma in County Hospital, and my daughter is sitting in hysterics two doors down."

Derrick lowered his gaze to the table. A coma? No, this wasn't happening. He shut his eyes and shook his head. "It was an accident. I'm sorry."

Winslow sneered down at him. "You haven't even begun to be sorry, but you will be. I'm going to make damn sure of that." He shoved back from the table and walked to the door, then glanced back at Derrick. "Make yourself comfortable," he said with a grin. "This is going to take a while."

The door shut and Derrick stared at the mirrored wall in front of him.

Minutes turned to hours, or so the clock on the wall said, and no one checked in on him. His head hurt from where it hit the steering wheel, and his wrists ached from the tightness of the cuffs. He twitched his cheek and it tightened from the dried blood. He leaned forward and rested his forehead on the table.

Time crept past. Another look at the clock indicated another half hour gone. He glared at the mirrored wall. "I have to go to the bathroom, please."

Nothing.

The more time that passed, the more his body ached. Again he looked at the glass window. "I think I need a doctor."

No response.

"I have to go to the *bathroom*."

His legs cramped. He needed to stand, stretch, pace, anything but sit here. Muffled sounds crept beneath the door. A woman's voice, angry and scared.

"Mom! Is that you? Mom!"

His parents barged through the door. Cori rushed to his side, dropped to the floor, and cupped his face in her hands. "Oh my God, Derrick. Are you all right?" She glared at the deputy. "Why is he here instead of the hospital? Can't you see he needs medical attention? And get these cuffs off of him, now!"

The deputy didn't answer.

"Your boy is fine, ma'am," Winslow said from the doorway. He nodded the deputy toward Derrick.

Wheeler helped Derrick to his feet and uncuffed him, then pressed him firmly down to his seat.

"He should be in a hospital," Cori said and straightened Derrick's shirt.

Derrick stiffened as his mother's eyes rose slowly from his shirt to his face. He shook his head slowly. "I wasn't drinking. Honest, Mom."

"Mrs. Anderson, this young man has caused a very serious accident while driving under the influence. And it's my understanding that one of my deputies offered him to go to the hospital and he refused." Winslow smiled down at Derrick. "Isn't that right, son?"

Derrick glared at Winslow.

Winslow moved to the chair at the table and motioned for Mr. Anderson to have a seat. "Deputy, bring in another chair for Mrs. Anderson, will you?" He turned his gaze on Derrick.

Mr. Anderson stood near the door and stared at Winslow through squinted eyes. "Whether he refused or not, he should have been brought to the hospital. He's obviously banged his head. Are you looking for a lawsuit, sheriff?"

Derrick tried to make eye contact with his father but Doug Anderson's red face and clenched fists said enough.

"Why weren't we called immediately?" Doug continued.

Winslow's eyebrows raised. "You were. My deputy tried to call you several times at the number your son provided. It wasn't until after a while when you didn't call back or show up that my deputy confirmed the number with Derrick, only to find out it was wrong. He called you again as soon as he could."

Doug huffed. "The wrong number..."

Winslow smiled. "Accidents happen."

Cori Anderson stood and put her arm around Derrick. "Come on, sweetheart, we're going to get you out of here."

Winslow stood tall and moved in front of the door. "I'm afraid that's not gonna happen, ma'am. Your son has been arrested for drunk driving. Now that you both have shown up, we can schedule a blood test, with your consent of course. There are also questions we have for the boy."

"Not without our lawyer," Doug said.

Winslow nodded. "Of course. I wouldn't think otherwise." Winslow grinned and walked to the door. "Might not be a bad idea to get the dogs in the pen together. As I understand it, Frank Larson has already contacted his. Ought to be interesting."

Dough Anderson moved toward his wife and son. "This was an accident." He looked down at Derrick and grimaced, then exchanged a concerned look with his wife. "And he is a minor. We're taking him home—"

"To the hospital first," Cori interjected.

Doug glanced at her. "And then home. If you need anything further, you can call us."

Winslow squinted at Derrick. "You want to tell me where you got the booze, son?"

"I wasn't drinking. I didn't have any booze."

"You want to explain how this all happened?"

"I already have at least a dozen times."

"Sheriff, you're walking a thin line," Doug Anderson said. "I said we're going to contact our lawyer. Your questions will need to wait until then."

Winslow nodded with a sigh. "Fair enough. I'll have my deputy draw up the necessary paperwork. Sign it, then you can go." He turned the knob on the door and then glanced back over his shoulder. "We'll need you and the boy, and your lawyer, down here first thing tomorrow."

"We'll be here," Doug said.

The door slammed shut and Doug glared down at Derrick. "Drunk, Derrick? You gave us your word."

Cori's eyes filled with tears. "You promised, Derrick," she said softly. "You promised."

"I'm telling the truth. I didn't drink. Belinda Larson threw her drink at me when I wouldn't kiss her," Derrick said.

"That's not the story Jess Winslow is telling," Cori said.

Derrick turned sharply at his mother. "She's lying. I don't know why, but she is."

Doug moved around the table and sat in front of Derrick, his eyes burning deep, and he had to struggle to contain the tone of his voice. "She says you invited them to the barn, that you supplied the alcohol. She says you knew Belinda liked you, so you teased her and coaxed her. She said you and Belinda argued about whether or not she could ride Arco."

"It's all a lie," Derrick said.

"She said Belinda wanted to prove to you she could ride him, so she went out to the barn and got on him."

Derrick tried to stand. "I'm telling you, it's all lies."

Cori fell back on her heels. "Derrick, stop. Sit down."

Slowly, Derrick did as he was told. "But it's a lie, Mom. That's not what happened at all. They came by on their own. I went out and told them to leave. Belinda was already drunk. I bet they went to Lloyd's party. You should check with the people there. I'm telling you the truth."

Doug sighed.

Derrick turned to his father. "What? You don't believe me?"

"Derrick," his father said, "The deputy has already confirmed Jess's story. He spoke to several kids at the party. They all said the girls weren't there."

"They're lying! I don't know what's going on, but they're all lying." Derrick dropped his chin to his chest and this time the tears rolled down his cheeks.

Cori stood and hugged him tight. "Doug, we have to do something."

The metal chair slide across the floor as Doug stood. "He did this to himself."

Derrick looked up with wet eyes and met his father's hard stare. "Dad, I'm telling you the truth. Please, can't you believe me? I haven't broken my promise to you."

The deputy returned and laid out the paperwork to be signed.

"That it?" Doug asked.

Wheeler nodded and grinned at Derrick. "Yeah, for now."

"Then get out of our way and let us out of here."

They stepped out into the humid late night air and Derrick paused as his parents walked ahead. Cori's heeled sandals echoed off the sidewalk. The quiet town slept while beasts roamed the streets. He among them.

Cori turned. The sadness slithered from her eyes to the ground like a black shadow and crept into his heart, squeezing the life from it. She held out her hand. "We'll call Will Chambers. He helped you the last time, maybe he can again."

Derrick descended the steps and wished more than ever that it was him lying in the hospital, or better yet, lying six feet underground.

Cori took his hand and squeezed with a sad smile in her eyes. Though she barely whispered, his mother's words bellowed through his soul. "Oh Derrick, what have you done to your life?"

CHAPTER ELEVEN

Cassie sat in the stall, her elbows on her knees, and rested her head in her hands as Arco lay beside her.

"This isn't happening," she choked.

"I'm so sorry, Cassie," Doc Lara Merrick said. "It's the most humane thing you can do for him now."

A whisper broke the air. *Let him go.*

"I can't. I...just can't," Cassie whispered back. She gazed up at Doc Merrick and pleaded. "Please don't make me do this. There must be something you can do." She reached out and gently stroked Arco's neck. Staring into his deep brown eyes, her resolve steeled. "No. I'm not going to put him down. Not yet." Cassie got to her feet. "Give me two weeks to nurse him. He can pull through this, I know he can."

Doc Merrick placed her hand on Cassie's shoulder. "He's suffering, dear. You're asking too much of him."

"He doesn't want to die right now. He wants to fight." Cassie glanced down at the heavily breathing animal. "And I'm going to help him do it."

Lara looked to Kate for help.

Kate put her arms around her daughter's shoulders. "I'm sorry, Lara, but this has to be Cassie's decision."

"Do you understand his injuries? He has a punctured lung, fractured snout, and permanent blindness to his left eye, a broken rib, and that's just to begin with. The most critical injury is his broken hock." Lara placed her instruments in her black leather bag and gripped it by the handles. "Cassie, even if, by some miracle, you pull him through this, he won't be able to do anything but live the rest of his days in the field." She took a step forward. "Do you understand what I'm saying?"

"Perfectly," Cassie said. "Now tell me what meds and the doses to give, and any other instructions I need to do this."

"You're a stubborn child," Lara said. "If you're not going to put him down, then he should at least be in a hospital."

Kate moved to the aisle and stood by the open door. "We can't afford a hospital. We'll have to do what we can from here."

Lara pulled a pad from her bag and scribbled across it. She tore a piece of paper off and handed it to Cassie. "Then you'll need these items as well as plenty of bandages."

Cassie knelt down and stroked Arco's neck. "And a whole lot of prayers."

Kate walked Lara out of the barn to her truck. "We appreciate everything you've done for us. Thank you, Lara."

"That little girl has chosen a journey that isn't going to end well, Kate. Prayers aren't going to help that animal now. You should have made this decision for her."

Kate glanced toward the barn. "Maybe you're right. But then maybe not." She returned her gaze to Lara. "Pray for her, will you?"

Lara opened the truck and got inside. She leaned out the window as she turned the key. She nodded at the barn. "That horse is as good as dead. My professional opinion is you're dragging on the inevitable and making the poor beast suffer for a young girl's sentimentalities. Think it over, Kate." Lara put the truck in gear. "Either way you choose, I'm only a phone call away. I'll help where I can. But it's going to take more than prayers to pull that horse through." She drove off and waved her hand out the window.

Cassie walked from the barn and stood by her mother, watching Lara's truck kick up dust down the long road. "Mom...thanks."

"I hope you know what you're doing, honey. Doc Merrick thinks you're making him suffer for nothing. Maybe you should really think this through again. I mean—"

"Mom, listen. I have thought this through. He can make it. He has to. I don't know what I'll do without him."

Kate stroked Cassie's arm. "I know, honey, but—"

"I have to believe that God will pull us through. Otherwise, what's the point?"

A new set of dust clouds emerged from the road out toward the main drive. "Who's that?" Cassie asked.

Kate held her fingers above her eyes to shield the sun. "I don't know," she whispered.

Cassie squinted against the sun and watched the large black SUV make its way up the winding road. It pulled up in front of Kate and stopped. A short, balding, round man exited the vehicle.

"Ms. Katherine Rhyne?" he asked.

"Yes?" Kate answered sheepishly.

He handed Kate a large envelope. "My name is Detective Joel Stevens. Mr. Frank Larson has hired me to investigate the accident."

"Investigate? Why?" Cassie asked. "Deputy Wheeler already questioned me about him. There's nothing new to say."

Detective Stevens smiled and bowed his head. "Mr. Larson just wants to take every step possible to assure that his daughter is treated fairly and gets what she deserves."

Kate huffed. "Gets what she deserves. Yeah, I'm sure Frank Larson is concerned that Belinda gets everything she deserves. Meaning my property."

"No, ma'am. Mr. Larson never mentioned anything about the land. He's just concerned—"

"Yeah, you've said that. I get it." Kate took a step toward him. "We weren't even here when the accident happened. We don't know the details."

Detective Stevens reached in his shirt pocket and pulled out a small notebook. He flipped it open and began to write. "What can you tell me about the Anderson boy?"

"He's a good boy," Kate said.

The detective smirked. "Now ma'am, I need a little more than that."

Cassie tsked. "What do you want to know? His shoe size?"

Detective Stevens flashed her a sideways glance. "How about whether he was a drinker? Ever see him drunk?"

Cassie huffed and Kate stepped forward toward the man. "Derrick is a good boy. He works for me and spends a great deal of his time here on my property. I have never seen him lift a bottle of alcohol, and I certainly have never seen him drunk. He does his chores, is polite, and is a well-mannered young gentleman."

Stevens chuckled. "Sounds like a real righteous lad, is that right?"

Kate nodded. "I'd say so."

"Then, I'd say you have some things to learn about your hired help," Stevens said with a nod toward Cassie. "And who you have buzzing around your pretty daughter, there."

Kate stepped back and put a protective arm around Cassie. "I'm well aware of who is 'buzzing' around my daughter, and I have no problem with the boy. If I were you, Detective, I'd be questioning Larson about his own daughter. Now that's a child with problems."

The detective folded the notebook and returned it to his shirt pocket. He nodded at the women and then opened the door to his SUV. He half-turned with one foot in the vehicle and his hand on the door. "What do you know about an accident the boy was in about a year ago?"

Kate and Cassie exchanged a look.

Detective Stevens smirked again and nodded. "That's what I thought," he said and got in the truck. He leaned on the door frame through the open window. "You ladies have a nice day, now."

Kate and Cassie stood in silence as they watched him drive away.

Cassie leaned into her mother. "I get the feeling those dust clouds he's stirring up are just the beginning of a storm."

"I think you might be right, honey," Kate said and squeezed

Cassie's shoulder. Again she gazed into the clear blue sky and shivered. "You just might be right."

CHAPTER TWELVE

Noah walked into the red barn and paused at the silence. It was as if the other horses sensed the closeness of death. Not a snicker, a movement, or even the low rumble of a whinny echoed through the barn. He made his way down the center aisle to the fifth stall on the right. Arco's stall. He held a small battery operated lamp up and peered through the metal bars on top of the stall door. It cast a soft glow against the night's darkness. The sight that followed choked him. Cassie sat in the hay with her back against the stall, her head tilted back on the wall with her eyes closed. Arco lay sprawled at her side with his head in her lap. Her fingers caressed the side of his face in a melodic, almost meditative rhythm.

Cassie opened her eyes. "Noah? Is that you?" she asked, squinting against the light.

"Yes, miss." He cleared his throat. "Your mom sent me to check on you."

Cassie's fingers pressed into Arco's fur and her lips quivered. "I'm fine."

"Your maw wants you to eat."

"I'm not hungry."

Noah slid the heavy door open and tossed a brown paper bag to her right. "There's a banana and peanut butter sandwich in there. I made it myself. And an apple." His eyes shifted to Arco.

Cassie's mouth curved only slightly. "Thank you, Noah. My favorite. That's very sweet of you. I'll try to eat it in a little while."

"It's after eight. I'm heading home now." He slid the door shut and looked in through the bars. "You call if you need me."

"Thank you. I will."

Noah left the big door open to the barn as he left. Poor kid. His heart ached. She was too sweet for this to happen to her. First her grandpa, then her father, now this. He shook his head as he got into his old Chevy pickup, rolled down the windows, and drove toward home.

###

He pulled up to the cabin, turned off the engine, and listened to the cacophony of night sounds of the bayou. A soft glow came from inside and the muffled voices of his sons, George and Hank drifted through the darkness. A moment later, Hank appeared on the rickety wooden porch.

Noah stared at the cabin, or so they called it. It had four walls. That was good. It had an indoor bathroom and running water. That was good, too.

Noah got out of the truck and slammed the heavy, creaking door shut. "Evenin', son."

"Paw," Hank returned with a nod.

Noah climbed the steps to the porch, careful to avoid step number three. He patted Hank on the arm and entered the cabin.

The insides consisted of one large room with a small refrigerator by the door, followed by a sink on the side wall and a toilet concealed by a shower curtain. They'd put up three-quarter high wooden walls — much like you'd find in a horse barn — to divide their sleeping quarters. On the floors of the bedrooms lay thick, green, military-style sleeping bags on top of old, mildewed twin spring mattresses.

George sat at the wooden table in the center of the room laying cards down in a slow, rhythmic motion. The glow of the lantern burned his face and cast dark shadows around his eyes.

Noah smirked. "You know, son, in the right light, you're one ugly 'n scary cuss."

George chuckled loudly at that. "Works in my favor, Paw."

Noah turned left and stepped toward the sink. He shoved some dishes out of the way and washed his hands. His mood shifted immediately. "Damn it, how many times I got to tell you to clean up after yerselves, you lazy asses? You're grown men, for crying out loud. Act it."

"Sorry, Paw," Hank said, and moved to clear the dishes.

Noah shoved him away. "Not now. Wait until I'm through. Get the hell out of my way."

George and Hank exchanged a glance. "Something wrong, Paw?" George asked.

Noah grabbed the towel hanging on the front of the sink and wiped his hands, his eyes fixed on the dishes. He threw the towel down hard on the counter. "I 'spose you could say somethin's wrong, yeah," he said with a slow nod. He leaned on the sink and stared at the water as it slowly disappeared down the drain. "There's been an accident. That's why I haven't been home. The young girl's horse was hit by a truck. Near dead. Little Cassandra is pretty broken up about it. Poor kid." He looked up in time to see Hank and George's exchange.

George stood and pulled his pants up with a wide grin. "Maybe I should head on over and convey my 'dolences to Kate," he said, and ran his fingers down his chin and throat.

"You scumbags. I can see the drool coming out your mouths."

"No, Paw, you got it wrong," Hank said. "We're sorry for the kid. I mean, first her father and now this. Good kid. Doesn't deserve it."

"No, she don't," George said. "So's maybe I should let Kate know we're here if she needs us."

Noah shot him a hard stare. "You'll do no such thing. Stay away from that woman."

George's face went solemn and Hank punched him in the shoulder. "Yeah, hang it up, Georgie. Kate ain't never gonna marry you. Now me, well, that's a different story."

Noah pulled a beer from the refrigerator and took a long drink, nearly downing it in one gulp. He burped and stared at the boys. "Neither of you scum are good enough for Kate. You stay away from her, hear me? You're never gonna get any of that property. It goes from her to the kid. It's not ours for the taking."

George groaned and dropped down into the wooden chair. "It ain't right, I tell ya. The old man should have left you some of that there land when he died."

"He did," Noah said. "What do you call this?"

George glowered up at him. "This? He gave you two acres of swamp thirty years ago, of which you managed to build this shack on."

"I built this cabin for me after your momma left. It wasn't meant for you. It ain't my fault she dropped you off here one day and disappeared. And it ain't my fault that neither of you ever made a life for yourselves. You've been living here free and clear all your lazy lives. You want better, go and get it. Do something constructive for a change."

Hank sat down opposite George and picked up the deck of cards. George reached for them but Hank pulled them away. He shuffled and then laid them down for solitaire. "We did try, once. Remember?"

Noah squinted in the shadows and his cheek flinched.

George snickered. "Yeah, it ain't our fault that Larson is contesting Cousin Miller's will." He smirked across the table to Hank.

"That will was a fake. I don't know what you boys thought you were gonna do with a fake will."

George nearly knocked the chair over when he stood. He turned around and pulled the refrigerator door open making the bottles of beer clang inside. He reached in and grabbed a Budweiser. "That property's ours. Fair and square. Old Man Miller was kin. Just 'cuz you was born to a whore mother don't mean we ain't 'titled to it. It's only right that it goes to us. Larson has no rights to it."

"My maw and paw never married. I have no claim to the property. Besides, Larson has money and he knows the will was a fake. He'll get the property in the end. And now he's going after the Rhyne land. All of it."

Hank drew in a quick breath. "What are you talking about?"

"The accident," Noah said. "His precious daughter was riding the horse when they were hit. She's in a coma. Might even die, looks like. He's going after the farm for damages. Kate was served today."

Hank looked incredulously at George.

George downed his beer and belched. "Welp, maybe it's time we do something about this thorn in our side. Larson has crossed the line too many times."

Noah shuffled his tired body over toward the bathroom. "And just what do you intend? We don't have the money to fight him, and neither does Kate. I feel real bad for them good people."

George and Hank again exchanged a glance. "Uh, yeah, right. Us, too. Kate doesn't deserve this," George said. "It was an accident. Everyone knows Larson has been after Rhyne Farm since before her husband died. Now he's going after both the Miller place and the Rhyne place. He'll own half the county if he gets it all. All we're saying is someone needs to put the brakes on him."

Noah shook his head. "You can't strong arm a man like him."

George shrugged. "Hey, all I'm sayin' is accidents happen."

Noah stepped into the light of the lantern and glared at George. What you sayin', boy? You gonna hurt the man?"

George stared at Noah for several moments and then smiled and shrugged.

"Wouldn't be the first time," Hank said with a chuckle.

Noah snapped a stare at him. "Who else you hurt?"

Hank flashed George a nervous look. George squeezed his lips tight, his eyes wide, and slowly shook his head.

Noah slammed his fist on the table. "Dammit Hank, you don't have to folla George like he were your meal ticket. I want to know what you know." His glare bore into Hank. "Who?"

"We ain't hurt no one," George yelled. "But Larson sure has. Hell, he murdered Cousin Miller and got away with it. Now he's gonna get away with his property, too. You don't see nothin' wrong with that? All I'm sayin' is something ought to be done, is all."

Noah grumbled and moved past the table to the first stall and crawled down onto the mattress, then crossed his arm across his eyes. "He ain't murdered no one."

"That's what you think," George said. "It's all over town. Cousin Miller was found dead with a pitch fork in his back. If that ain't murder—"

Noah stirred. "But no one ain't point a finger at Larson. It was a bad robbery. The police says he must've come on the men and surprised them. Case is closed."

"I can't believe you willin' to just roll over and take it. We bein' robbed by this here political bull ding." George grabbed the back of a wooden chair and flung in across the room.

Noah didn't open his eyes. "You disrespectin' me, boy?" he asked menacingly. He listened as the door creaked open and then slammed shut, followed by silence.

CHAPTER THIRTEEN

Frank Larson sat beside the bed and gently grasped the delicate fingers of the girl who lay before him. He pulled them to his quivering lips and closed his eyes against the pain that raged within his chest, then bowed his head in silent prayer.

The door opened and the light from the hospital corridor darkened the woman as she stepped into the gray room. "Frank? When did you get here?" she asked. "I thought you were working out at the Coleman's site today." She crossed the room to the window, set her purse on the windowsill and then moved toward the bed.

Frank cleared his throat and fidgeted in his seat. The sight of his daughter lying before him threatened to release all that he'd worked so hard to contain. He stood and offered his chair to Ruth Ann. "I went earlier this morning. My men have things under control, so I figured I'd stop in here to see how she was doing." He moved to the window and leaned against the wall.

Ruth Ann sat where Frank had been and resumed the vigil at

Belinda's bedside. She stared at her daughter's sweet, still face. Without moving her gaze, she said, "Tom Burgess phoned this morning. He said the Rhynes have been served."

"Good."

Ruth Ann turned in her seat and faced him. "Why? It was an accident. Why are you going after those poor people?"

Frank pushed away from the wall. "What the hell you mean, accident? Their horse almost killed her. Look at her! That vegetable in front of you is your daughter, and you're concerned about *them*?"

"All I'm saying is that they're suffering, too. That poor girl's horse is near dead and you know as well as I do that they just don't have the money to pay these bills. And we don't even need their money."

Frank's face reddened with anger and his eyes bulged. He lowered his voice and spat the words through gritted teeth. "I'll take their whole farm before I let them get away with this."

Ruth Ann stared at him, and then shook her head. "That's what this is all about, isn't it? You've wanted their farm all along, and now you're stooping so low as to use your own daughter's accident as an excuse to go after them for it."

Frank huffed and waved her away. "You can think whatever you want. All that matters is that someone pays for what they've done to her."

Ruth Ann stood and stepped in front of him, then picked up her purse from the windowsill. "You're already destroying the boy that hit her, and his family. Isn't that enough? Because of you, that boy may be going away for years."

"No. It isn't enough. It'll never be enough." Frank moved around her and sat in the chair near the bed. He stared down at Belinda and trembled. "And you'd do well to sort out your emotions into their proper perspective."

Ruth Ann walked to the doorway and stared back for a long moment. "That child lying there needs her father. She needs you, Frank. She doesn't need money or revenge. She needs you."

Frank watched Belinda's still form. "Money and revenge are all we have left."

"Then I've lost you both; Belinda to this horrible accident, and you to your rage and greed."

The door clicked closed. Frank cleared his throat to dissolve away the lump that had formed, and shrugged his shoulders to loosen the tightened muscles across his back. "I'll make things right by you, Belle. I'll make them pay." He stood and leaned over her and kissed her gently on the forehead. "Sleep well, my dear."

###

Belinda tried to move her lips, open her eyes, or lift a finger, but nothing worked.

Daddy, wait! Don't go. I can hear you. Please. Look at me. No, wait! I agree with you. I understand. Look at me. I'm awake. I'm here. Can't you see me? Please!

But no matter how hard she tried, she couldn't force movement. Mentally exhausted, she lay paralyzed and listened as her father softly shut the door. Silently she screamed. A tear fell from the corner of her eye.

Do it, Daddy. Make them pay for what they've done to me.

The door opened and someone bumped the bed.

Who's there?

"Good morning, Belinda. I'm Nurse Avery and I'm here to check your vitals."

Something tightened around Belle's arm and she knew it had to be the blood pressure cuff.

"Everything looks great, right where it should be. You know, you really need to wake up. Your parents are so worried about you." Nurse Avery tapped her arm gently.

I'm trying to wake up, but I can't. Why can't I move? Why can't I see? Why can't I speak? Oh, God! What's happened to me?

Silent screams filled her head as she cowered in a corner of her mind.

CHAPTER FOURTEEN

Cassie stood by the bay window in the living room and stared out at the north pasture. Memories of Arco grazing beneath the weeping willow by the brook forced tears to form. She shook it off and faced her mother. "It's been five days and Arco doesn't seem to be getting any better. What else can I do?" She gripped the back of the dining room chair and clenched her jaw. "I don't know what to do."

Kate held a solemn expression.

"Mom, no. I can't." She grasped her upper arms tight to shield herself from the attack of sobs that welled within.

"Cassie, I know how hard this is for you."

"Do you? I mean really, do you?"

"Yes. I've been where you are right now."

Cassie stared at her mother as thoughts raced through her mind. "Did you kill him?"

Kate bowed her head to the letter in her hands. "Her. And no, I didn't kill her. I put her out of her misery. I had no choice. Just like you—"

"I have a choice!" Cassie said, and spun away toward the window. "Just because you didn't try to save your horse, doesn't mean I won't do everything I can to save mine."

"That's not fair, and you know it. You weren't there. I did try. I prayed, and cried, and administered medicine. I changed bandages and slept in her stall for over a week. But in the end, I had no choice. I'm sorry, Cassie, but things don't always work out the way we want them to. Sometimes God has other plans."

"I don't believe that. If God wanted to take him, He would have, and not made him suffer so much."

"Maybe He is trying to take him, but you won't let him go," Kate said, her words gentle but sharp.

"Why would He make me do this? Why do I have to make this decision? I don't get it! This isn't fair. Is this one of God's almighty lessons that you speak about? Is this the God they preach in church as just and kind?" Cassie wiped at her tears with the back of her hand. "Then why?"

"I'm sorry, sweetheart. I don't have those answers. But you mustn't lose your faith in God. Even if…no matter how this turns out, you must remember that God is with you and He will see you through."

"No! If He lets this happen, if He makes me kill Arco, I will never walk with Him again. Do you hear me? Never!" Cassie moaned with pain and raced to the door.

Kate called out her name, but Cassie didn't stop. She slammed the door behind her, the windows shaking from the force. She jumped from the porch and ran toward the barn.

"God, are you listening?" Cassie asked through shaken words. "You can't do this. Please. I'm begging you. Please help Arco live."

Two hours passed before the barn door slide open and Kate's voice carried through the silence.

"Cassie? Honey? Are you in here?"

Cassie stroked Arco's head in her lap. "Yeah, I'm here."

Kate appeared at the stall door and gazed down through the bars. "Are you all right?"

"Yeah, I'm fine." Cassie continued to stroke Arco's cheek. "Hey, I'm sorry about that scene back there."

"No. Don't apologize. I understand."

Cassie gazed up at Kate. "Yeah, I guess you really do." Arco huffed and fidgeted. "How old were you? I mean, when you had to put your horse down?"

Kate moved inside the stall and kneeled down by Cassie. "Her name was Charlotte. I named her after the spider from Charlotte's Web. I was fifteen. We were living in Kentucky at the time. We had just had a wonderful run out in the fields, much like you and Arco do. I'd hosed her down and then released her in the field to graze." Kate smiled with a distant gaze. "A terrible storm came up out of nowhere. At least that's how it seemed to me. Before I knew it, Grandpa had me by the arm and was pushing me down the bulkhead of our basement toward my mother who was already inside. I tried to tell him that Charlotte was out in the field, but he said there was no time." Kate's eyes fixed on the steady motion of Cassie's hand as she stroked Arco's cheek.

"Mom? Are you okay?"

Kate blinked several times. "I'm sorry," she whispered. "My father was right. There wasn't any time. Within minutes, a tornado barreled through our farm, ripping up trees, fences, and even our tractor. It took out the barn and tore a path straight across the field."

"Oh my God. Charlotte?"

"We found her lying in the field with a tree across her body. At first, I thought she was already dead, but I prayed with every step I took that she was somehow alive. And she was, but barely."

"What did you do?"

"My father went back to the house and got his gun. When he came back to the field, all I remember is screaming that I'd make her better. I begged him to give me a chance. My mother had to lead me away."

"But Grandpa didn't shoot her, right?"

"No. When I asked him years later why he didn't, he said he couldn't do that to me. He said it had to be my decision, or I'd never be able to live with her death. I needed to reconcile, he said." Kate slid the stall door open, then knelt down beside Cassie. "Two days passed and I began to think she may be getting better. But that night, when I went to check on her, she had blood oozing from her nostrils and mouth, and her breathing was shallow. Our vet was more than two hours away." Kate's voice drifted as she stared down at the dark horse lying before her.

"What happened?" Cassie asked, her heart tight from the tears in her mother's eyes.

"I went back to the house and got my father's rifle, loaded it, and returned to the barn."

"You shot her? By yourself?"

Kate smiled weakly. "Yes."

"But, why didn't Grandpa do it? Why didn't you make him?"

"It wasn't his place, Cassie. It was my decision. My responsibility. She was my horse, and it was only right that I be the one to release her from her pain."

Cassie stared down at Arco with wide eyes. "I'm not as strong as you, Mom. I can't shoot him."

Kate caressed Cassie's hair. "You don't have to shoot him, honey. When it's time, you'll call Lara. She'll put him down quietly, with a needle. He'll just drift off to sleep."

"When it's time," Cassie repeated. She wiped at new tears and took her mother's hand. "If you don't mind, I'd like to be alone with Arco for a while."

"Sure, sweetheart. I'll start a small dinner for us. Come up to the house whenever you're ready." Kate stood and gazed down at Cassie, then to Arco. "I love you," she said, then stepped out and slid the door behind her.

Cassie waited until the outer barn door slid shut before she let the sobs hiding in her throat escape. The pain was like no other. Her soul screamed out and fought against the gripping anguish as it twisted and writhed within her body. "I love you, Arco," she sobbed into his neck. "With my whole heart. I know you're fighting this fight for me. You will always be my warrior."

She covered her face with her hands. "Spirits of the Mist, please help me. Come to me. I need you. Grandpa Joe, if you're out there, help me." She rested her head back against the stall wall. "Daddy," she whispered, "I need you now more than ever." She closed her eyes and chanted, "Spirits of the Mist, come to me," over and over.

Moments passed that seemed like hours, but then a faint, cool moist air crept along her skin.

"Are you there? Is that you, Spirits? If so, I pray to you. Help Arco, please, I beg you. I can't lose him."

You have to let him go.

"Oh, please, I *can't*. Please don't make me do this." The broken words fell from her lips. Cassie caressed Arco's cheek and stared down into his face. "Tell me what you want me to do."

Exhausted, Cassie lay down beside Arco, her head upon his neck, and drifted into a reckless sleep.

Arco stirred beneath her and Cassie pushed herself up. "Easy, boy. Shh, easy."

Arco struggled, his breaths hard, his nostrils flared. Sounds escaped him, and Cassie thought she could almost hear him moan.

"Oh, Arco. You have to be still."

His body twitched and she realized he was shaking. The painkillers were wearing off. She tried to stand but Arco laid his head in her lap.

"I'm going to get you some more medicine. I'll be right back." She held his head gently and started to slide her leg from beneath it when she saw the shiny liquid in his nostrils. Slowly, she reached out and touched it. "Red. Oh, no. No! Oh my God." She looked down into Arco's wide, pained eyes and her heart shattered.

Cassie wrapped her arms around his neck and buried her face in his fur. "I'm so sorry, boy. I've been so selfish. I just can't let you go. What will I do without you? Who will ride the fields with me? Who will I tell my secrets to? You're my best friend, Arco. My life will never be the same. I love you so much. I will never get over losing you. You will be in my heart forever. I promise you." She kissed his cheek and sobbed. "I wish I could die instead of you."

Slowly, she calmed her sobs and steeled herself. She reached into her jeans pocket and pulled out her cell phone. With shaking fingers, she pressed the speed dial number four and waited.

"Hello?"

Cassie choked back her tears. "Dr. Merrick? It's time." She disconnected the call and stared down at Arco. "Shh, my brave friend. It'll all be over soon." Again the sobs came. "I love you so much. Oh, God, it hurts so much! I'm so sorry. I'm sorry I left you alone. I'm sorry I wasn't here. I should have been here. Please forgive me."

A truck pulled up outside the barn door about twenty minutes later, and a moment after that the large door slipped open. Footsteps approached and Lara appeared at the bars of the stall.

"Hi, honey. I came as fast as I could."

Cassie didn't respond.

Lara slid open the stall door. Cassie looked up and stared at the black leather bag in her hand. "Is it in there?"

"Yes."

Cassie's squeezed her eyes shut against the pain. She grabbed a fistful of mane and her sobbing, her shaking body hunched over Arco. "Then do it."

Lara kneeled down beside Arco and Cassie, and laid her hand gently on Cassie's arm. "I'm so sorry, honey. You're doing the right thing." She reached in her bag and pulled out a needle filled with clear liquid. She held it to Arco's neck.

"Wait!" Cassie said. She bent forward and kissed Arco gently on the cheek. "Here's a kiss for you to take to heaven. Remember me, as I will remember you. Always. I love you."

Lara released the liquid into Arco's neck and sat back on her heels. Moments later, Arco's struggling slowed. Moments after that, he lay still, his head resting quietly in Cassie's lap.

Her tears stopped and Cassie sat motionless, staring down at Arco's closed eyes. "He's gone, isn't he?" she said, knowing the answer before she asked.

Lara laid her hand on Cassie's shoulder.

"Leave me alone, please."

The outside door slid shut with a soft thud, and Cassie listened for the sound of Lara's truck driving away. She lay her body alongside Arco's and draped her arm over his neck. "I'm so sorry. I miss you so much." She buried her face deep within his mane and cried like she'd never cried before.

CHAPTER FIFTEEN

Cassie sat in her little red Ford Focus on Barrington Street and stared across at the beige house with brown shutters like she'd done every night since that day. For the past week, all she'd been able to do was cry, throw up, and cry again. Her mother said she needed to get over this, that she did what had to be done. Really? She must be crazy. Because to her, this was only the beginning. The beginning of a new, dark, cold, and lonely life. The tears were gone, all cried out, used up. Her heart...well, that was gone, too. Revenge was now her new life source.

A light flickered in the upstairs east window and a shadow crossed the room. *His* shadow.

Cassie glanced at the clock on the dash. A little after nine. She'd been here almost an hour, trying to drum up the strength to confront him—the destroyer of her world. She closed her eyes and laid her forehead against the steering wheel. How many more nights would she have to do this? The talk around town confirmed his guilt, at least to

Cassie, but she still wanted to hear it from Derrick's own lips. Rage coursed through her body and she gripped the steering wheel with both hands. She stared up at his room through narrowed eyes. She had to get out of here.

Cassie turned the key to start the engine and jumped from the knock at the window.

"Hey, you okay?" Derrick said.

The insides of Cassie's head whirled and she wondered if she could pass out while sitting. She stared at him, frozen in place. She wanted to scream, but a part of her was almost happy to see him. Up to this moment, she thought she wanted him dead. She hated herself for the thought, but she felt it nonetheless. But now, with him standing before her, something changed. "Yeah, I'm fine," she managed to say.

Derrick tried the door handle. "Can I come in?"

Cassie's throat tightened. She looked up at the full moon in the dark sky and shook her head. Would the cosmic cruelty ever stop?

She eyed Derrick as he stood smiling outside the car, one hand resting on the roof, the other on the door handle. She fought the urge to put the car in gear and speed off, against the hope that it would catch him off guard, that he wouldn't let go, that he'd be dragged beside the car, and…

Instead, her fingers pressed the unlock button on her driver's side armrest and released the gate to hell.

Derrick slid into the seat beside her and she wanted to gouge his eyes out. He fidgeted with his hands in his lap. "I've called."

"Yeah. I know." Something white outside her window caught Cassie's eye, and she turned to see an old woman with a small white dog stepping quickly beside her, its tail and head held high. Any other time she would have thought this was cute, adorable, and sweet, but now she found it irritating. "How stupid," she mumbled.

Derrick raised his eyes to the woman and the dog. "I think it's cute."

"You would." Cassie glared at him. "You didn't just kill the only true friend you've ever had."

Derrick's face paled. "Oh my God, Cassie, I'm so sorry. I didn't know. Honest. I've tried to call but your mother just said you weren't ready to talk to me. She never said that he…" Derrick's gaze dropped to his lap. "She never said."

"Would it have mattered? Would anything be different? Arco would still be dead."

"Cassie, I'm—"

"Don't," Cassie said, and held up her hand to stop him. "Don't you tell me one more time that you're sorry. It doesn't mean anything to me. It's a lie."

Derrick shifted in his seat to face her. Cassie was surprised by the depth of pain she saw in his eyes. Her resolve to hate him wavered at the sincerity in them, but the hatred quickly returned as the image of him and Belinda played in her mind.

"But I am sorry. You'll never know how true it is." He continued to stare at her. "If I could take his place, I would. Do you think I want to live knowing the pain I've caused?"

Again, Cassie's feelings surprised her. She'd thought a hundred times that she wished it was Derrick dead instead of Arco. But now that he said it, her stomach tightened with regret. She wanted to tell him not to think that way, but the other side of her—the cold side—only looked away.

"Hey, do you think we could go for a drive? I don't want my folks to see me sitting out here. I'm sort of on house arrest. I'm not allowed out without one of them being with me."

Cassie faced him. "What happened, Derrick? Why did you do this?"

Derrick closed his eyes and shook his head. "I know what you've probably been told, but I don't think it's the truth."

"Really. So you think my own mother would lie to me?" *It wouldn't be the first time*, she thought.

Derrick glanced toward his house. "No, not if she believed what she'd been told. But the story that's going around isn't true." He looked at her and reached for her arm. "Come on, let's go for a ride."

Cassie shrugged away from him and glanced at the clock on the dash. "It's almost ten. I have to get home or my mother will worry."

"Just a short ride. You need to hear my side. Will you at least listen?"

Cassie faced front and stared out the windshield at a brown dog peeing on the car parked under the streetlight. Finally, she turned the key and started the car. "Whatever. I doubt seriously you'll have anything to say that'll change how I feel," she said, then headed down the street.

"You may be right, but I have to try."

Derrick's voice was soft and beaten. Again, compassion for him edged under her skin, and again, she became angry with herself for her weakness.

A short time later, Cassie pulled off the main road to Willow Tree Lane, the dirt road that skirted Rhyne Farms. And shortly after that, she pulled off the dirt road into the field where she parked under the weeping willow tree.

She glanced over at Derrick, then released her seatbelt and got out of the car. She walked to the brook and looked up at the moon in the sky. Derrick was right. She needed to hear his side, to know why. She needed to have him look her in the eye and tell her why he betrayed her love, and why—oh, why—he killed Arco.

But, he hadn't killed Arco. Not really. Because of him, she'd been forced to do it. And for that, she hated him more than words could ever tell. She shook against the anger and wished for the release of tears, but none came.

The full moon shone brightly and reflected in the slow moving water before her. The night was warm, but Cassie wrapped her arms around herself and shivered from the cold within.

The car door shut and she closed her eyes. "So, tell me," she whispered, "I need to know. Why did you betray my feelings? Was it just a game?"

"No. I didn't betray you."

Cassie snickered. "Sleeping with some other girl is betrayal in my book, let alone it being my worst enemy."

"I didn't sleep with her, I swear. Nothing happened, Cass."

"That's not how Jess tells it. She said you called Belinda and invited her to the barn for some Fourth of July drinks. Jess went with her because Belinda asked her to. She said when they got there you were pretty buzzed and took advantage of Belinda. She said you even winked at her before you led Belinda into the house." Cassie's eyes burned from the sting of dry tears.

"It's all a lie. None of it happened like that," Derrick said, his voice low and steady. "Does it even sound like me?"

Cassie spun around and nearly bumped into him. "Really? Why? Tell me, why would she lie when her best friend is lying in a coma in the hospital because of you?"

"Exactly."

"What?"

"She's lying because her best friend's lying in a coma because of me. She wants me to pay. But it wasn't my fault. And Jess is covering up for what really happened. I don't know why, maybe she thinks Belinda would get in trouble for stealing the horse and she's making some whacked out attempt at protecting her. Or maybe she just doesn't want people thinking any worse of Belinda than they already do. Maybe in some crazy way she thinks she's doing Belinda a favor."

"Fine. Then go ahead and tell me what really happened." Cassie stared hard into his eyes and expected him to look away. But he didn't. Instead, he stared straight back without a flinch.

Derrick cleared his throat and swallowed hard. "Lloyd had a party, that's true. But that's where the truth ends. The girls were at that party. I'm sure of it."

"How are you so sure? Everyone there said they never showed."

"Because David told me they were. Only, I can't tell anyone he told me. Larson can cause his family a lot of grief if I do."

Cassie squinted up at him. "But, if he's your only source of the truth, don't you think he'd want you to tell? I mean, what sort of friend would let another take a fall like this when they could stop it?"

"He was going to, but I convinced him not to. I don't want to see his family hurt because of me. I've already hurt enough people." Derrick stepped back and faced the brook. He reached for a pebble and tossed it in.

Cassie shook her head. "All right, whatever. I'm still listening."

"I was sitting in the guest house watching TV. It was just after nine. I know, because I had just put a movie on and made some popcorn. I heard a noise coming from the blue barn. I went to the intercoms, like you showed me, and heard voices. I looked out the window to see if I could see a car or make out who was up there, but I couldn't. So I got in the golf cart and drove up." He sat on the ground near the brook.

Cassie sat down beside him. "And?"

Derrick rested his arms on his knees. "Belinda and Jess were there. Jess was standing near the car and Belinda was in the barn near her horse's stall. She was holding a bottle of Captain Morgan in her hand. She was drunk…plastered."

"What did she say?"

"I don't remember all the words that were spoken that night, but I remember telling her they needed to leave. Jess and I helped her out of the barn and she tried to kiss me. When I said no, and pushed her away, she got angry. Real angry. That's when she threw the open bottle of liquor at me and it spilled on my clothes. I think I said something like, 'they had to leave,' but I can't remember, exactly."

"So, you weren't drinking?"

"Not a drop."

"But, the police said you were drunk. They said you didn't pass the Breathalyzer."

"They lied. I told them what happened, but they didn't believe me. Apparently you were right, Larson is a very powerful man. For all we know, he owns the cops."

Cassie scoffed. "Yeah, maybe, Anderson, but I doubt he owns the sheriff. Since you ki—I mean, since the accident, Larson had my mother served with papers. He's trying to sue for our farm."

"You mean the whole place?"

"Yeah, every last inch. My mother is devastated, but she's a heck of a fighter. She got us the best lawyer our money can buy, which isn't saying much. Thing is, we don't have the kind of money that can buy a lawyer nearly as good as Larson's. She's trying, though."

"Cassie, I'm so—"

Cassie gave him an angry stare and Derrick grimaced. "Anyway, Derrick, how did she get her hands on Arco? I mean, if you were right there, how'd she do it?"

"I left. I got back in the cart and drove to the guest house. I was getting ready to change my clothes when I heard a horn beep, and it sounded like it came from near the red barn. I looked out the window and saw Belinda on Arco and Jess yelling at her to stop. I ran out to stop her, but she kicked me away and took off. Jess told me she was heading to Miller's place."

"Oh my God. Miller's?"

"Yeah. And she was riding up through the north pasture. I remembered about the quicksand. I knew I had to stop her. That's when I got in my truck and drove around the back road after her. I wanted to head her off. But it was raining and the roads were wet." Derrick's voice cracked and he closed his eyes.

"Go on, Derrick. I need to know."

"They ran out from the woods. I couldn't see them until they were right in front of me. Arco tried to rear, but she was yanking on his mouth. I slammed on the brakes and my truck swerved, but..." Again, his voice cracked.

"Derrick, I..."

Derrick pulled her to him.

Cassie pressed her hands against his chest to stop him. She pulled away and moved toward the car. "We need to go. I have to get you home and then get home myself before my mom freaks."

"Cassie—"

"Thank you for telling me your side."

"Do you believe me?"

Cassie didn't answer. She slid into the driver's seat and waited for Derrick to get in the car. They drove back to Derrick's in silence.

Derrick tapped the dashboard lightly as Cassie pulled onto his street. "Stop. I'll walk to my house from here. I need to sneak back in."

Cassie kept her eyes focused on the steering wheel without speaking, but she could see him watching at her from the corner of her eye.

Derrick sighed and got out of the car. He rested his arm on the roof and leaned in. "Thanks for letting me tell you my side. It means a lot."

Cassie glared at him. "Derrick, you misunderstand. I appreciate you telling me. I needed to know. But I don't forgive you. I never will." She turned away and focused on the road ahead of her.

"Maybe one day you will. Until then, I guess there's nothing left for me to say." He stood back and shut the door but paused a moment longer. "I love you, Cassie."

Cassie mumbled softly in return, "I hate you."

CHAPTER SIXTEEN

Derrick stood on the side of the road and watched as Cassie slowly drove out of sight, and out of his life. He felt as if he were to drink all of Lake Eerie he'd never quench the dryness of his soul. He walked up the road and stood in front of his house staring up at the tree just outside his window. Screw it," he said, and proceeded up the stairs to the front door. He entered the house and faced his father's blank stare.

"What the… where the hell are you coming from? You're not supposed to be out of this house without one of us being with you. You know this," Doug Anderson said.

Derrick waved him off as he climbed the stairs to his room. "Yeah, I know this."

"You get back down here. I'm not through with you."

Derrick stopped and stared hard at his father. "Yeah, well, I'm done with you. I'm done with all of you!" he said, and stomped the rest of the way to his room.

Cori Anderson emerged from the hall bathroom next to Derrick's room. "Derrick? What's going on?"

"Ask him," he said, and slammed his door shut. His parents' raised voices drifted under his door.

"Let me talk with him," his mother said, and then there was a soft knock on his door.

"I'm not into it right now, Mom. Really."

"Derrick, please. Just give me a few minutes."

Derrick gritted his teeth, but moved to the door and pulled it open. "What?"

Doug pushed his way past Cynthia into Derrick's room. "I want you to sit and listen," he said.

Derrick clenched his jaw and glared at his father, but didn't move.

"I said *sit*." Doug said.

"Derrick, please do as your father asks."

With all the calm and reserve he could muster, Derrick moved to the bed and sat at the edge of the mattress. "So. I'm listening."

Doug pulled the chair from the desk and sat down in front of him. "First, I don't appreciate the attitude. We've been more than fair with you, after all you've put us through."

"All I've put—"

"Yes. We've tried to give you the benefit of the doubt, but you've made that pretty hard to do."

"Dad, you've never trusted me ever since… that night."

" That's not true. That night happened over a year ago. We've put that all behind us when we moved here. And we did this to give you a fresh start. Isn't that what you asked for? And then you pull this?"

"Doug, please," Cori said, and reached for Doug's arm.

"No, Cori, he needs to hear what we have to say."

"But we didn't, did we?" Derrick said.

"We didn't what?" Doug asked.

"We didn't leave it all behind us. I've never had a fresh start, because you've never forgiven me for killing Daniel."

Cynthia gasped. "Derrick, please!"

"Please what, Mom? Please don't mention the accident? Please don't mention Daniel's name? *What?*"

Doug stood and hovered above Derrick, glaring down at him. "Don't you speak to your mother like that."

"But it's true, isn't it? Neither one of you has forgiven me. I might have killed your son, but he was my brother. Did you ever think of that? Don't you think I wish it had been me who died? Every single day I wish it. And this," he waved his arms around the room. "This isn't a fresh start, it's a freaking prison!"

"How dare you speak like that in this house?" Doug bellowed.

"But don't worry. You won't have to deal with this *problem* of yours much longer. Pretty soon they're gonna put me away, and I'll be nothing but a stale memory to you both."

Cori burst into tears. "Oh Derrick, no one's going to put you away. We're not going to let them," she said, and looked hopefully at Doug. "Tell him. We're not going to let that happen."

Doug stood over Derrick with tight lips. "He'll get what he deserves."

Derrick stood and crossed the room. He needed space. He needed air. "See what I mean?" he said to his mother. In one quick motion, he reached for the door and ran from the room.

"Derrick! Stop! Where are you going? Stop!" Cori yelled.

"Don't worry, I'll take care of all your problems for you," he called over his shoulder. He was halfway down the stairs when his father exited his room, and he was out the door before either of them could reach him.

CHAPTER SEVENTEEN

Cassie pulled into the drive and headed up the winding road toward her house. She glanced at the dashboard clock. 11:45. Not good.

She climbed the stairs to the front door, turned the key in the door lock, and carefully slipped inside.

"Cassie? Is that you?" Kate appeared in the hallway, arms crossed, her head slightly tilted to the left.

"Sorry, Mom."

"Where have you been? I've been worried sick. I've called three of your friends looking for you, and I was just about to call the police. You know better than not to call."

Cassie made a tsk sound and moved past her mother. "I said I was sorry."

"Really? You're sorry? And that means everything is fine now, right?"

"What do you want me to say? Sorry is all I have." Derrick's face flashed in front of her, and her words came flooding back. *Sorry doesn't mean anything to me*, she'd said. She stopped in the middle of the hall and faced her mother. Kate stood, arms at her sides, with hurt on her face. Fragments of Cassie's already broken heart crumbled in her chest. "Mom, really. I didn't mean to worry you." Cassie went to Kate and hugged her.

"I know, honey. I'm sorry to attack you like that. It's just…you know. Things have been crazy around here. And I'm worried about you. You don't seem to be getting any better."

"But I am. I talked with Derrick tonight." Cassie moved away and walked to her room. Kate followed.

"Did he tell you his side of the story?" Kate asked.

"Yeah." Cassie dropped down on her bed.

Kate sat at the corner of the bed and brushed Cassie's hair with her fingers. "And how do you feel?"

"Not good. How else should I feel?"

"All right, then, let's start with, did you believe him?"

"Yeah. Nothing happened between him and Belinda. It really was an accident. He was trying to help." Cassie's voice lowered to a near whisper. "He was trying to save Arco."

"What about him being drunk?"

"He wasn't. He didn't even have a drink. Belinda threw her open bottle of Captain Morgan on him." Cassie pulled her stuffed rabbit with the long floppy ears from her pillow and played with his paws, and then looked at her mother. "He's innocent, Mom."

"Did you tell him you forgave him?"

Cassie lowered her gaze to the rabbit on her lap. "No."

"But, you—"

"I told him I hated him."

"Oh, honey. That boy is going through so much. He really could use a friend right now, with all the trouble he's in." Kate rose and walked to the window. She folded her arms in front of her and stared out into the darkness.

"What do you mean?"

Kate turned. "Honey, Mr. Larson has managed to get him tried as an adult."

"No! They can't do that." Cassie jumped to her feet and threw Mr. Flopsy to the floor.

"I'm so sorry, sweetheart. They can, and they will. It seems they aren't listening to the same story you heard tonight. In their eyes, he's guilty."

"How much time does he have?"

"He's scheduled for court the week after next. If he's convicted, he'll go to an adult correctional facility. The judge will decide for how long, but I think minimum would be three to five, providing Belinda doesn't pass away. Without getting them to believe the truth, I'm afraid he hasn't got a chance."

Cassie dropped back down, her shoulders hunched forward. "Maybe he deserves it."

"You don't mean that." Kate moved to her. "Cassie, you don't mean that."

Cassie threw herself back on her bed and stared at the ceiling. "I don't know what I mean! I'm so confused. Part of me hates him, but part of me feels for him, too. You should have seen him. He looked so…broken." She sat up and stared at Kate. "Isn't there something we could do?"

"Like I said, other than getting someone to come forward with the truth, I can't possibly see what else."

"How about Roger? Do you think he would look into it?"

"Roger is having difficulty enough trying to keep this farm and these lands for us. And he's not a criminal lawyer, Cassie. I'm not sure he could help him, even if he wanted to."

"He has to at least try. Mom, we can't just let him go to jail. He's innocent." Cassie stood and paced in front of her bureau. "I don't get it. Why aren't his parents doing anything?"

"They are. They don't have a lot of money left. They've hired the best they can afford. And the real truth of it is, they don't believe him."

"What do you mean? They're his parents! How can they not believe in him?"

Kate returned her gaze to the window. "Because they've been down this road once before." Kate's eyebrows furrowed and she spoke low and even. "Cassie, Derrick had a car accident a year and a half ago. His brother was thrown from the car. He died, sweetheart."

Kate's words stole Cassie's breath. Killed someone? Derrick? "But, if he killed his brother, why isn't he in jail?" she whispered.

"Because he had an expensive lawyer who proved it was an accident."

"He never said anything about this." Cassie reached down and picked up the rabbit from the floor without thinking of what she was doing. "Was he innocent? I mean, do we know that for sure?"

"I only know what his mother told me. There was alcohol in the car."

"You spoke with his mother? When?"

"Three days ago." Kate said.

"Why didn't you tell me?" Cassie stood and waved her arms. "Why is everyone lying to me? I can't believe this."

"I didn't tell you because I didn't want to upset you more than you already were."

"Oh, please. Give me a break. Really, Mom? Like you didn't want to upset me when Grandpa suddenly died, or when my dad supposedly drowned? Did it ever occur to you that it might bother me more to keep me in the dark? That maybe I wanted to be there at the hospital before they put my father six feet under? I didn't even get to see him. You stole that from me."

"I'm so sorry, honey."

"Then you promised you'd never lie to me again. And now?"

"Cassie, I didn't lie to you. You've been so upset over the accident. I just—"

"So you decided to keep this huge secret from me? How could you? We made a deal. No secrets!" Cassie stepped toward Kate and glared at her. "Oh, I get it. That is, unless you feel otherwise. Nice, Mom. Now I have no one left to trust." She rushed to her door and yanked it open.

"Cassie, wait. Where are you going?"

"Out," she said, and ran from her room.

Kate followed behind her. "You can't. I forbid it. Cassie, please! Stop. Don't go out like this."

Cassie made it to the front door and slammed it shut behind her.

###

Kate stood in the middle of the hall. Cassie was right. She'd betrayed her daughter once again. She wrapped her arms around herself, dropped to her knees, and sobbed. Minutes passed before she realized she hadn't heard Cassie's car. She went to the window and looked out toward the red barn. There it was. *Oh thank you, Lord.*

An hour passed. Kate threw on her slippers, walked to the barn, and slid the heavy door open. A dim light shone from Arco's stall. Her heart thudded louder with every footstep.

She stopped outside the stall and peered inside. A small battery operated lantern sat against the far corner wall. There, so sweet and small, lay Cassie, curled up on a clump of hay in the center of the stall, her head resting on Arco's burgundy halter, asleep. Kate turned to leave, and then noticed something else. Held tight against Cassie's chest, folded in her arms, was a braid made from Arco's tail.

Kate covered her mouth to hold back choked sobs. "Oh, my sweet baby." She turned away and closed her eyes. She returned to the house and stepped up onto the porch, then turned toward the woods. "If you exist, if you're out there, I pray to you spirits of the mist. Please help my baby girl."

CHAPTER EIGHTEEN

Three Weeks Later

Mid-day held the thickness of humidity and a heavy haze floated in the air. Though the temperature stood near eighty-eight degrees, a cold chill ran through Cassie's bones. She wandered through the downtown city streets of Grenada, glancing inside the storefronts unseeing. What had she done to deserve all this? Was this punishment for some major cosmic screw up?

Cassie stepped off the curb to cross Grandview Drive and jumped as a car sped past with a blaring horn. She shook her head to clear the fog. When she refocused, she stood before the Grenada Lake Medical Center.

Cassie stared at the ominous three-story glass-fronted structure and wondered which floor Belinda was on. Visions of Belinda standing at her window staring down sent an edge of discomfort through her and she placed her palm against her stomach to settle it. *She's comatose, idiot. She doesn't know anything anymore.*

She looked left, and then right, then proceeded more carefully. She paused before the looming building, then opened the front glass door and approached the information desk. She didn't speak; only stared at the lady behind the counter.

"May I help you?" the lady asked.

"Um, well, I…"

"Miss, may I help you? Are you sick or injured?"

"No. I'm fine. I…I want to see one of your patients."

The woman began typing. "Patient's name?"

"Belinda Larson."

"Your relation to Miss Larson?"

"Friend," Cassie heard herself say.

The woman typed a few moments more. "Yes. Miss Larson is in room 303 on the third floor. Here. You'll need to wear this visitor's badge while you're visiting."

Cassie took the badge and slipped it over her head.

"The elevators are to your right and down that hall," the woman said.

Cassie smiled. "Yes. Thank you."

The elevator doors opened on the third floor and Cassie stood frozen, looking out into the corridor. The doors closed and the elevator began its decent. When they opened next, she was back on the main floor. She closed her eyes and inhaled deeply, and then pressed the number three once again.

The doors opened and Cassie stepped out into the corridor on the third floor. The bright lights and shiny white floors made her think of Heaven in a bizarre sort of way. She remembered a story she'd heard of a woman who had claimed to die and pass through the white light. She'd described a bright light and long, white corridor with glowing, blurry shadows of people standing at the end, waiting for her. Cassie shuddered at the eerie resemblance.

"Are you all right, miss? Can I help you find someone?" a nurse asked.

Startled, Cassie jumped and shot her a nervous smile. "No, thank you. I'm good. I think it's… I think her room is…um."

The nurse returned her smile. "Why don't you tell me what room you're looking for?"

"Number 303."

"Oh, sure. That's just right down this hall. It will be your fourth room on the left. Miss Larson, is that right?"

"Yes," Cassie said, and then started down the hall. "Thank you."

"My pleasure."

Cassie read the numbers of the rooms as she slowly passed each one until she reached room 303. She paused outside the closed door. Reaching for the door with a shaky hand, she pushed it open and peeked around it as it slowly exposed the room within. The drawn curtains darkened the room against the mid-day sun and the soft glow from several machines allowed shadows to creep around inside. A bed dominated the center of the room, flanked by two faux leather green chairs. Cassie edged her way in and flipped the light switch by the bathroom door. A tall nightstand stood beside the bed and contained a telephone, a plastic water jug, a box of tissues, a couple of plastic cups, and a Get Well card laying on its side. Cassie walked to the nightstand and poured a cup of water. Absentmindedly, she stood the card upright to face Belle.

Belinda's body looked small and frail as she lay motionless beneath the white blanket and sheets. The monitors hummed and bleeped in song with her heartbeat. Cassie winced. Her anger and hatred dripped away, replaced by compassion and empathy as she stared down at the helpless girl. Reflex made her reach for Belinda's hand.

Who is it? Is someone there? Speak so I can hear you. Who's there? Belinda spoke to the darkness of her mind.

Cassie pulled a tissue from the box on the nightstand and blew her nose. She sat down in the chair and gazed at Belinda. "What a sight you are," she said with a cracked, dry voice.

Who is that?

"I don't know why I came here. Maybe I thought I would give you a piece of my mind. But it looks like you have your own things to deal with."

I don't recognize your voice. Please. Keep talking. Don't go away. Please. Are you from my school?

Cassie stared without speaking. She took in every inch of Belinda's pale face. Faint bruises remained, but there was no swelling or cuts. "The good news, if there is any, is that your beautiful face has remained unscarred," she scoffed.

Really? I thought for sure my face was a wreck.

Cassie closed her eyes and rested her forehead on the cold metal sidebar of the bed. "I should just go. I don't know why I came."

No! Please don't go. Not yet.

Cassie's gaze drifted to Belinda's face. "Why did you do it,

Belinda? Why'd you take Arco like that?"

Cassie? Belinda filled with anger at her recognition. *Get out! Why are you here? I don't want you near me. Look at me! This is your fault. I'm trapped in this other dimension and it's your fault! Get out! Do you hear me?* Belinda screamed silently.

"Derrick said you were drunk. How could you think of doing such an awful thing?"

Don't you mention that name near me; I don't ever want to hear his name, or yours, ever again!

Cassie huffed. "You know, part of me hates you, but part of me feels sorry for you." A small creak made her turn.

"What are you doing here? You, of all people, don't belong here."

Cassie stood and stared at Jess. "Why not? None of this is my fault. She did this to herself."

Are you crazy?! I didn't do this, Derrick did!

Jess took a step toward Cassie. "How can you say that? Do you honestly think any of this is her fault? It was bad enough that your freak of a horse spazzed out on her. She couldn't handle him, and he took off through the woods. But I told Derrick not to go after her. I told him! And he went anyway."

"He told me he was trying to save her. It's a miracle she even made it through the north pasture without falling into any quicksand. If she had made it across the street to the other field, she would have fallen in some for sure."

Jess eyed her with disgust. "You're defending him? After everything he's done?"

"No. I mean, yes. No, I'm not defending him. I'm just telling you what he said."

"He's lying."

Cassie moved around Jess and stood at the foot of the bed. She stared down at Belinda and shook her head. "I thought so, too, at first. Now I'm not so sure. I think I believe him." She set her gaze on Jess. "If I'm wrong, then you tell me the truth."

Jess sat in the chair that Cassie vacated, took Belinda's hand in hers, and stared at her. "You already know the story. I've told it a hundred times."

"No. I know what the sheriff says, what Mr. Larson says, what my mother says, and what Derrick says, but I haven't heard what you have to say. Tell me, directly to my face."

Jess glared at her.

Cassie stood in disbelief. "Jess, really? You're willing to let Derrick take the fall for all of this? Why?"

"Look at her. Have you ever seen anyone so helpless? She needs my support. Even if she made a bad decision, she doesn't deserve this. Does she?"

Cassie shook her head slowly.

Jess's face hardened. "But Derrick does. It should be him lying here, not Belle. He's done this before, you know. He killed someone in a car accident a year ago. I heard my father talking to Mr. Larson. Did you know?" She smirked. "No, I bet you didn't. Forgot to share that little secret, did he?"

"You're wrong. I do know." *Because my mother told me, not Derrick,* Cassie thought. She refused to show the dread that crept through her veins. "What about me and my mother? Do we deserve what this family has, and still is doing to us? She stole my horse. For what? Because she couldn't get Derrick to like her? And now her father's using her as an excuse to go after my family's land. We're losing everything because of her."

Jess shrugged her shoulders. "It is what it is."

Cassie grunted and moved toward the door. She glanced once more at Jess. "Her stupid act of jealousy has put her in this position. But you're right. She doesn't deserve this. And you know something? Neither does anyone else. She's managed to destroy her family's life, my family's life, and Derrick's family's life." She looked past Jess to Belinda. "If she could be aware of anything at all, I wish it would be to know that."

"Yeah, well, I think Derrick's doing a pretty good job of screwing up his own life even more."

"What do you mean?"

"I'm sure you know. He's gone. On the run. When my father catches him—and he will—he'll be doing his waiting for trial in a nice little ten-by-ten cell."

"Where did he go?"

"Duh. If we knew that, then Daddy would have brought him in by now. No one knows. It's been two days. You mean you didn't know, either? Not much of a boyfriend, is he?"

Cassie rolled her eyes. "Whatever. I'll find him." She pulled the door open and started out.

"I wouldn't get any more involved with him, if I were you. Daddy's going to find him, and if he finds out you helped Derrick in any way, you'll pay for it."

Cassie looked back. "Really? Did you know that Arco's dead?"

Jess stared through wide eyes.

"Yeah, your friend there did that, too. So tell me, do I really have anything left to lose?" Cassie waited a moment longer and then left the room. She needed out, and fast. She walked briskly down the hall toward the elevator as her back pocket began to vibrate. She pulled her cell phone from the pocket and glanced at the caller ID. Unknown Number.

"Hello?"

"Cassie, it's me. I'm sorry to call, but...I need your help."

CHAPTER NINETEEN

Cassie pressed the cell phone to her ear as she rushed to exit the hospital. "Derrick! Where are you? Are you crazy? You need to—"

"Cassie, slow down. I'll explain everything. Can I see you?"

"Where are you?" she asked. "Are you still there?"

"Yeah. I'm at the brook by your barn, up by the willow tree."

Cassie huffed. "You've got to be kidding. Haven't you caused enough trouble for my family? If the sheriff finds you there, my mom will be in trouble big time."

"Relax. No one will find me here. Not unless you tell them. I'm out by the brook in the north field. Will you come?"

Cassie closed her eyes and took in a deep breath. "I guess. I don't know what you think I can do for you. You really should just turn yourself in. This was so random."

"I don't need to hear this from you right now. Just meet me, will you? Like I said, I'll explain when I see you."

"I'm just leaving the hospital. I'll be there in about thirty-five minutes."

"The hospital? You mean you went…never mind. I'll see you then. Um…think you could bring me a dollar burger from McDonald's?"

"You're pushing your luck."

"Yeah, I guess. Hey, Cass, don't tell anyone you've talked to me. Please?"

The cold Cassie said to turn him in. The cold Cassie wanted revenge. "I won't," she said and hung up.

Cassie drove down Main Street and headed out of town. She stopped at the intersection as the light turned red and smirked. The large golden arches of McDonald's graced the sky across the street on the right. For a moment, she swore it glowed neon and flashed. "Fine, Derrick. I'll get your stinking burger."

She left McDonald's drive-thru, slid the bag to her lap, and then pulled back onto Main Street. The city—if you could call a hospital, a police station, a fire station with two trucks, a post office, and some clothing stores with a couple of fast food joints spread about a city— faded in her rear view.

Within a matter of twenty minutes, Cassie found herself on comfortable and familiar rural roads heading toward Rhyne Farms.

Cassie pulled down the dirt road toward her house and then took the left onto Willow Tree Lane and out to the north field. Kate was giving a lesson in the arena next to the blue barn and Cassie hoped she hadn't seen her before she had a chance to get under cover behind the thick woods that lined the road.

She drove through the winding trail until it opened to the north pasture. The late afternoon sun burned high in the sky and cast dark shadows beneath the large weeping willow. Cassie pulled the car up and parked beneath the tree, then walked to the brook and glanced around for Derrick. On the far side of the brook where the woods continued, Cassie heard the sounds of branches cracking. Moments later, Derrick stepped out.

"You make enough noise," Cassie said.

"Yeah, well, being a fugitive isn't exactly my forte."

"No. It seems car accidents are."

"Touche." Derrick hopped across the brook on several large stones. He reached her and stared down into her face. "I tried to tell you. Honest. But it just never seemed like the right time."

Cassie huffed and moved around him. "So, what do you want from me?"

"A burger would have been nice, but—"

She nodded. "Go look in the car."

Derrick leaned in the driver's side door and pulled the bag from the front seat.

"Oh yeah, I sort of ate the fries. Sorry," she said with a shrug.

"No worries. Thanks for this," he said, and ate the burger in two bites.

"God, did you even taste it?"

"I'm hungry."

Cassie's heart softened and a tinge of guilt crept in for eating his fries. "I'm sorry. You must have been terrified out here alone all night. What have you done for food?"

"I've been drinking the water from the brook. And, believe it or not, I even caught myself a fish," he said, and stood a little taller with a smile.

Cassie couldn't help but smile. "Good for you. A real Grizzly Adams, huh?"

Derrick chuckled. "I'm not sure who that is, but he sounds like a mountain man, so, yeah." He walked to the edge of the brook and sat down. "I also hit the vending machine in the red barn."

Cassie's anger replaced her momentary warmth, and she dropped down heavily beside him. "Are you crazy? What if someone saw you? What if my mother saw you? Do you know how much trouble I would have gotten in?"

"You haven't done anything."

"Do you think they'd believe that? We were a couple!"

Derrick flinched. *"Were* a couple?"

Cassie focused on the water. "Derrick, with everything that's happened...I mean...a lot has changed, you know?" She pulled his ring from her finger and held it out to him.

He folded her fingers into his hand. "I love you. That hasn't changed."

Cassie's eyes glistened. "What do you want from me?" she whispered.

Derrick cleared his throat. "I'm sorry. I don't want to upset you."

Cassie shot him a hard and watery stare. "Really? You have a funny way of not upsetting me since that's pretty much all you've done since we met."

"Really. Sorry you see it that way." He moved a step away from her and shoved the ring in his front pocket. "Okay, look. I was hoping you'd help me get to the bottom of all this."

"Why'd you run away in the first place?" Cassie asked.

Derrick tossed several stones into the brook. "Because I overheard my father talking to Sheriff Winslow. Seems Larson got his way. I'm to be tried as an adult."

Cassie stared at the ground. "I know. Mom told me."

"Yeah. And you know what that means? I'm going away. For a long time." He shifted to face her. "My life will be over. I mean, you might as well kill me now. It'd be a better fate than sitting in jail for the next…however many years."

"They can't do that," Cassie whispered.

"They can, and they are. So you see? You're my only hope, Cassie. I need you to get Jess Winslow to tell the truth. I need her to come forward. That's the only way I'm going to get cleared." He took hold of her hands and stared down at her. "I'm innocent. You have to believe that."

"Why'd you run, then? That was stupid. Now you look even more guilty."

"I had to. My parents don't believe me. They watch me like the Gestapo, so using the phone was out. I'm not supposed to leave the premises without one of them with me. My home was more like a prison than anything else. How was I supposed to get a chance to clear my name? I had to leave. I knew it would be the only way I could talk to you and try to convince you to help me."

"I don't know, Derrick. Larson is causing so much trouble for us. I don't want to bring more crap down on my mother. I'm not sure she could handle it."

Derrick squeezed her hands and took a deep breath. "You're my only hope. Without you, there's nothing left for me to do. I can't show my face anywhere. The minute I do, I'm done."

Cassie pulled away from him and stood. She stuffed her hands in her back pockets and glared at him, gnawing on her bottom lip. "Dammit, Derrick! This is so unfair."

Derrick lowered his gaze and closed his eyes. His shoulders slumped slightly forward and Cassie's heart ached for him.

"It's all right, Cass. I understand if you don't want to help me. You're right. You've got enough to deal with."

"It's not that I don't want to help you. I do. It's just... I don't want... I can't... Oh, you know what I mean! This sucks." Cassie stomped to the car and leaned against the front of it with her arms crossed. Derrick followed.

"I know."

"What are you going to do in the meantime? You can't stay out here."

"I'm good. I'm sort of getting used to it," he smiled.

"Yeah, well I won't be able to sleep knowing you're stalking these woods. It's amazing you haven't been sucked up by the quicksand, or worse, eaten by an alligator." Cassie glared at him and shook her head. "You are such and idiot. Sneak into the red barn tonight. You can sleep in the loft. But, whatever you do, don't come down. I'll try to bring you some food after my mom is asleep."

"You don't have to do that. I don't want to cause your family any more trouble."

Cassie rounded the vehicle to the driver's door. She pulled it open and said, "You don't have a choice. Just do it. If you don't, I'll come out here looking for you, then I'll fall into quicksand and drown, then you'll have to live with that."

Derrick rolled his eyes. "You really know how to drive home a point. Okay, I'll be there. So, does this mean you're going to help me?"

She got in behind the wheel. "I'll see what I can do."

Derrick leaned on the door. "I love you. And not because you're going to help me." He moved closer to the window. "I just love you."

Cassie stared into his eyes. "I'll help you, Derrick, but then we're through." She put the car in gear. "I'm sorry."

CHAPTER TWENTY

Wednesday morning came, and Jess started the day the same as every other day over the past three weeks. She walked her dog, stopped at the bakery on Seventh Street, and then drove to the hospital to spend the morning with Belle.

Jess walked quietly into the hospital room and stood beside Belle's bed. She stared for several moments, and then shook her head and stomped over to the window. "Okay, this is enough. You need to wake your lazy ass up," she said, and yanked the heavy burgundy and teal striped curtains open wide. "Do you see that? It's called the sun. And you look like you haven't seen it in years." She returned to the side of the bed and sat in the chair. Her voice softened. "Come on, Belle. I can't stand being here without you. You're my best friend."

I'm trying, Jess. Really, I am.

A young nurse entered the room, glanced at the open curtains, and smiled. "I'm glad you did that. She needs to feel the sun, even if she can't see it."

"Do you think she's aware? I mean, do you think she can tell the difference between day and night? You know, light and dark?"

Yes. I can tell the difference in the shades behind my eyelids.

The nurse moved to the opposite side of the bed and took readings from the machines. She checked the IV tube, and pressed a button on the monitor. "I think so."

Jess gazed at Belle. "Do you think she'll ever wake up?"

Of course I'm going to wake up! Don't you even think I'm not. I have to. I just have to.

"Honey, these are questions for the doctor. You really should ask him."

"I've tried. But no one will give me a straight answer. The doctor speaks to me like I'm a child. I'm sixteen. I can handle something more than, 'your friend's body has shut down to care for itself.' Really? No duh! And her parents won't talk about it. Not to me, anyway." Jess walked to the window and stared down at the parking lot. "What's your name?"

"Rachel."

"Please, Rachel, can't you tell me anything?"

Rachel glanced down at Belinda and then motioned to Jess. "Why don't we go and get something to drink? I'm about due for my break, anyway."

Jess smiled. "Thank you."

No, don't leave. Talk here. I want to know, too. Don't leave. I need to know if I'm ever going to wake up from this nightmare. Please!

Jess pulled a Coke from the cafeteria vending machine and sat at a table by the row of long windows. Rachel chose a small bag of Doritos and an apple juice from the counter and joined her. Jess waited patiently as Rachel opened her chips and juice.

Rachel leaned forward in her seat. "I'm not really supposed to discuss this stuff with the loved ones. This is the doctor's area of expertise. But, I'll tell you enough to help you understand a little better. My best advice is for you to do some research on your own."

"Thank you. I really appreciate this."

"Okay. First, there's a Glasgow Coma Scale that we use to determine the severity of the head injury. It determines the conscious state of the patient on a scale from three to fifteen; three, being the most severe and fifteen being the most normal. Belinda is between three and eight."

"She's severe. So what's that mean? Is she just a vegetable?"

"No, not at all. It means that her body is trying to repair the damage enough to be able to sustain itself. Many, many patients come out of this state with a full recovery."

Jess took a long sip of her Coke. "Many, but not all."

"Yeah, that's right. Every person and circumstance is unique. There's no way of knowing which patients will come out of it and which won't."

"So, can she hear us? Does she even know she's alive?"

Rachel offered some chips and Jess shook her head.

"Okay, look. For the longest time, it was believed that people in a comatose state couldn't hear or feel anything. But recent studies show that this is incorrect. People tell stories about their experiences while in a coma, and many say they heard and felt their loved ones around them. They were able to recite conversations that took place, and describe a feeling of touch." Rachel leaned forward and rested her arms on the table, her eyes wide with excitement. "There's a report of a man named Ron Houben who, doctors discovered, was one of these coma patients who had a normally functioning brain after twenty-three years! Imagine that? He'd been a captive in his mind for twenty-three years and the doctors didn't even know. It's amazing he didn't go mad!"

"Oh my God," Jess said, and her stomach flip-flopped.

Rachel seemed to realize her callousness. "Oh, I'm sorry. I'm not saying Belinda will be in a coma that long."

"Then what are you saying?"

"I'm just saying that there's hope for a fair chance of recovery. And that it is quite possible that Belinda can hear and feel. I think you should talk to her. A lot. Tell her everything that's going on with you, your friends, and her family. Everything and anything that would help to stimulate her."

"I have been talking with her. You really think she knows what I'm saying? I mean, her parents seem to think she's totally brain dead. Have you seen them with her? They're like death's angels just waiting for her to die. I can't stand it. It makes me sick. I leave every time they show up." Jess sat back and shivered against the warmth of the room.

"I can understand that. I haven't seen Mr. Larson with her, but her mother has come in several times on my shift. I know what you mean. I've suggested she talk with Belinda, but she doesn't seem to know what to say. She just sits there staring through the saddest eyes I think I've ever seen. Heartbreaking, really."

"Yeah."

"Okay, I have to get back," Rachel said, crumbling her chip bag. "Are you going to be all right?"

"Yeah. Thanks for this. You'll never know how much it means to me. I'll do what I can to help her."

Rachel rose and smiled down at Jess. "I have no doubt you will. You're a really good friend. See you around."

Jess remained at the table and stared outside at the late morning shadows. A bitterness tugged at her taste buds. All those conversations she'd been having with Belle, all those private thoughts she shared when she thought she couldn't hear; now it was possible she did hear. Everything.

Several hours passed and Jess prepared to leave. "Okay, Belle, it's time for me to go. I promised my father I'd stop by the police station on my way home." She placed the TV controller on the nightstand. "I hope what Rachel says is true. I hope you can hear me, and feel me near you, because I'm about ready to shake the crap out of you. I can't take this much longer. I need you here. You're my best friend." Jess squeezed her hand. "No one else knows what you've done for me, how you've helped me get through my parents' divorce. You're a good person, Belle. I know you care about things, about people." She lifted the bedside bar and locked it into place. "Anyway, my biggest fear is that when you wake up you're going to hate me." Jess's eyes filled.

I don't hate you.

"I know I lied. I did it to protect you. Okay, the truth is I did it to protect myself. I had to. You put me in a really bad situation. If I tell the truth I know the court will send me to juvie. My dad won't be able to do anything to stop it this time." Anger edged between her words.

"That was a really brain dead thing you did, Belle. Really? Stealing Cassie's horse? And then galloping off to the swamp in the middle of the night? Thanks for pulling me in the middle of this." She stared down at the helpless shell before her and her heart softened once more.

"Sorry. I guess you're paying your own price for your stupidity." Jess lifted Belle's hand, straightened the sheet around it, and then placed it gently on the bed. "Anyway, I'll come by again tomorrow." She walked to the door, shivering at the eerie stillness that had filled the room. "I have to go meet my father for lunch."

Jess sighed. "You're like a sister to me, Belle. I'll make it up to you, I promise. I'll do whatever it takes to protect you. So, don't worry, the truth will be between us...oh, and your father. I had to tell him."

My father? Why would you do that? That wasn't so brilliant. I guess you really do need me to keep you from acting stupid.

###

Deputy Robert "Bob-O" Thompson smiled as Jess passed his desk. "Hey, kiddo. Nice to see you."

Jess smiled back. "Same here, Bob-O. Is my father in his office?"

Bob-O shook his head. "Nope. He left about an hour ago. Don't know where to. He had Councilman Larson with him, though."

Jess furrowed her eyebrows. "Oh, okay."

"Everythin' all right?" Bob-O asked.

"Yeah, it's just that he asked me to stop by on my way home from the hospital. He wanted to have lunch with me. Not a problem. I'll catch him at home. I'm just going to headphones from his office. Thanks."

Jess rummaged through the papers on her father's desk searching for her headphones book without success. She made to leave and caught sight of a folder marked "Anderson." With a quick glance around, she closed the blinds in her father's office, careful not to alert Sarge. She opened the folder and pulled out the first set of papers. Deputy Wheeler's report of the accident.

Jess skimmed through the Collision Narrative to the part where Wheeler gave the Breathalyzer. "Mr. Anderson appeared shaken and off balance. Due to the smell of alcohol, a Breathalyzer test was administered which read .08 on the scale," she read aloud. "As Mr. Anderson refused ambulance transportation to the hospital, and believing Mr. Anderson to be under the influence of alcohol, it was my opinion to arrest Mr. Anderson."

So, it was true. Wheeler falsified the Breathalyzer. But why? Jess closed the file and put it back where she found it. She went to the glass window and slowly opened the blinds. The coast was clear. She left the office and headed down the hall toward Bob-O.

"Forget something?" Bob-O asked.

"Huh?"

"Didn't find your headphones?"

Jess smiled. "Oh, no, I guess not. My father must have brought it home. Have a good one."

"You too," Bob-O said with a wave.

CHAPTER TWENTY-ONE

Jess wasn't surprised to see her father's police cruiser parked in the driveway, but Deputy Wheeler's cruiser made her pause. *That scumbag's in my house.* She passed the deputy's car and pulled into her driveway beside her father's car.

She entered the house and headed down the stairs to her sanctuary—the basement. She'd done it all, from cleaning the clutter to mending walls, and finally, painting. In the end, it was hers. Her parents wanted to give her Jason's room when he went off to college last year, but Jess insisted on the basement. It was far enough away from them to give her a sense of freedom from their constant arguing. Now that they'd divorced and it was just the two of them, it was far enough away from him, too. She resented her father; it was his fault her mother left to begin with. He was a hard man, her mother always said so. No one, including Jess, could live with him. But her mother didn't want her; she said she wasn't set up yet to handle a teenager, and that it would be best for Jessica to stay with her father so her life wouldn't have to change. Little did her mother know…everything changed anyway.

Jess opened her bedroom door, threw her purse on her bed, and then stopped and strained her ears at the sound of male voices coming from the floor above her bed. She returned to the main floor and slithered along the hall toward her father's den. As she got closer, the sliding doors off the kitchen leading to the backyard opened and Deputy Wheeler walked in, talking on his cell phone. Jess leaned against the wall behind the large mahogany grandfather clock out of his view. The door to the den stood kitty-corner across the hall. The voices coming from the room were stronger and louder. Jess made them out to be her father's and Mr. Larson's.

Jess peeked with one eye around the clock as Deputy Wheeler took an apple from the wicker basket on the center island and sat on one of the barstools. He tossed the apple in the air while he listened, and then took a crisp bite. "Yeah, but I don't want anything to go wrong this time, you hear?" he said through crunches. "I've been doing all the dirty work so far. Now it's your turn." He took another bite and glanced down the hall in Jess's direction. He squinted and then said into the phone, "Yeah, I have the Breathalyzer… Of course it'll stick. I did it myself. Those things are pretty easy to fix, if you know what you're doing." He slid off the stool and paced around the kitchen.

The grandfather clock chimed and Jess gasped. Deputy Wheeler's head jerked up and he stared toward the hall. Jess pressed herself against the wall as hard as she could and hoped he couldn't see her around the side of the clock.

A moment later she heard him say, "No, nothing's wrong.

Everything's good. You just get Drakes to do his part. I have the stuff on Larson. This is worth a hundred K a piece. Don't screw it up. Okay, I'll catch up with you later at the club. Yeah, the Sports Pub."

The sliding doors opened and then closed. Jess waited before daring to peek around the clock. When she did, he was gone. Over the sound of her heartbeat, Jess concentrated on the voices coming from her father's study.

###

"Listen, Frank," Tom Winslow said, "it wasn't my idea to press charges against this kid. This is your doing."

"My doing or not, you're the sheriff and I expect you to act like it. You never should have let him wait out his trial date at home. That boy should be behind bars. And now look. He's been missing for five days and you don't seem any closer to catching him," Frank Larson said. "He's out there gallivanting around like nothing ever happened."

"I doubt the kid is living like nothing happened," Tom scoffed. "Don't worry, we'll catch him."

"You better be right about that. I've gone through a lot of trouble to make sure he pays for what he's done."

"If everything my daughter says is true, the boy will be punished accordingly. Only, I have to tell you, she seems a bit sketchy at times. But I trust her to do the right thing once she gets on the stand."

"Wait a minute. Jessica is going to testify?"

"Of course," Tom answered. "Is that a problem?"

"Uh, no, not really." Frank crossed the room and stood in front of the fireplace resting his glass on the mantle. "Have you talked to her? Do you know for sure what she's going to say? Has she said anything about—"

"Yeah, we've talked." Tom's eyebrows furrowed and he gazed at Larson through narrowed eyes. "You got something else to tell me?"

Larson cleared his throat. "No, of course not. I just want to make sure she doesn't screw things up. That's all. I don't think it's a good idea to have her testify. She'll be shaken up by being on the stand. She might say something that isn't true."

"The boy was drunk. My deputy did a Breathalyzer. The kids at the party already confirmed my daughter's story. She's just going to tell it like it happened."

Larson drained his scotch, placed the glass down on the mantle, and walked across the room. "Yeah, well you just make sure she does."

"Are you threatening my daughter, Larson?"

Larson glared at the sheriff. "Just sayin'."

"I think you're saying more than you're saying."

###

Larson's boots echoed on the wooden floor as he approached the door. Jess's heart pounded in her chest, and sheer fright froze her in place. The doorknob rattled and shocked her into motion. She ran back to the front door, opened it, and then slammed it shut. "I'm home," she called out.

Frank Larson entered the hallway and faltered. His eyebrows furrowed and his quizzical stare made Jess's stomach tighten.

Sheriff Winslow exited his den behind Larson. "Hi, honey."

"Hi," Jess said, her glare steady with Larson. She turned toward her father. "I'm going down to my room." And then back at Larson. "Have you seen Belle today?"

"No, not today," Larson said.

"That's not surprising," she mumbled.

He opened the door and Jess glanced out at the deputy leaning against the white and black squad car. He smiled with a nod. Her mouth dried and she jogged down the stairs toward her room to avoid looking Larson in the eye.

She overheard Larson at the top of the stairs near the door. "Just make sure nothing goes wrong." The door slammed shut for the second time.

Jess went back upstairs and called to her father. Tom stood at the side window near the door and watched Larson as he drove away.

"I don't like him and I don't trust him," she said.

Tom faced her. "Since when? You've always spoken very highly of him and his family. I thought Belinda was your best friend."

"She is. And that was before the accident. Do you know that he hardly ever goes to see her? Mrs. Larson is there all the time, but he never goes."

"Some things are harder for some people to deal with than others."

Jess scoffed. "I don't think that's his problem."

"No? Then what is it, if you're so smart?"

Jess chewed at her bottom lip, and then moved down the hall toward the kitchen. "Never mind. You're probably right. I'm hungry."

The door opened and closed, and when she looked back her father was gone. Jess sat at the center island in the kitchen, pulled a red Fiji apple from the fruit bowl, and toyed with it in her hand before crunching down into its crisp pulp. She stared out the window and chewed slowly. Derrick didn't have a chance in hell of getting off.

Larson was right. He'd certainly gone to great lengths to make sure Derrick paid. But if she blew the whistle on Wheeler and the false Breathalyzer, then she'd blow the whistle on her own lies. And what about Wheeler? What was he up to? How did he have Larson over a barrel? Nothing made any sense. She shrugged. Whatever. That was between them.

She had plenty of problems of her own that needed solving. Like what was happening to Derrick and Cassie…well, it wasn't right.

She bit down into the apple once more, her father's words playing in her mind. *I trust her to do the right thing.* Had he really said that? Since when did he ever trust her? Jess's stomach tightened. He believed in her. She never knew he felt that way. She shook her head. How was it possible to hate someone and love them, too?

He was right, though, she had to tell the truth. Too many people were being made to pay for her and Belle's mistakes. She had to come clean. She had to face the consequences. A year in juvenile detention might go by fast. Then she'd work on cleaning up her act. Then she'd work on making him proud.

CHAPTER TWENTY-TWO

Deputy Wheeler nodded and walked past the bouncer at the door to the Sports Pub. Two men sat at a round wooden in the back by the pool tables, drinking beers. Wheeler made his way through the crowded, smoky room, past the three-man band playing *Paradise* by Coldplay—and doing a decent job of it—along the bar toward the back room. Two young ladies, a brunette and a blond, sat at the bar and smiled as Wheeler passed. He smiled and nodded. "Evenin' ladies."

The brunette batted her eyes and placed a hand on his chest. "Hey, handsome. Care to buy me a drink?"

Wheeler grinned. "Would love nothin' more than to do just that, but got some business to take care of first. Stick around. Wait for me." He winked, kissed the tip of her nose, and moved on to the two men at the round table where a beer sat waiting for him. "Thanks, boys," he said as he skidded the chair out and sat.

A muscular, tattooed man of about thirty-five, wearing a jean jacket with the sleeves cut off and an old, dusty black cowboy hat, leaned his chair back on two legs and guzzled down his beer. He placed it heavily on the table and wiped his mouth with his sleeve. "So, what you think Larson is gonna say when he hears we want his money?"

"I think he'll pay right and willingly," the other man, tall and thin, said with a chuckle.

"Not askin' you," Cowboy said.

Wheeler sipped his beer and then leaned forward on his forearms. "I agree with Slim. I think he'll pay without a hitch. We have too much on the man for him not to."

"I'm thinkin' he ain't gonna be so easy to scare. That falsified Breathalyzer isn't enough to shake 'im up. He'll just say you did it on your own without his telling ya to," Cowboy said.

Wheeler rolled his eyes and sat back. "You are one dumb slug. The Breathalyzer is just the beginning. We have the death of Old Man Miller, and the death of Cassie's father both on Larson's hands."

"I don't get it," Slim said. "Larson didn't kill them men."

"He may not have ordered them dead, but he hired the man who was supposed to scare them out of their land. This little plan of ours, the one we're here to discuss, this will be the final piece to set Larson up good and plenty. He's loaded, and this election means too much for him not to pay." Wheeler waved toward the waitress for another beer. "Besides, we're being generous. We're not asking for more than he can afford. We're only pinching his belt a bit, not breaking him." He glanced between Cowboy and Slim. "You did set things up like we talked about, right?"

Cowboy smirked. "Yeah, it's been set up." He nodded at the far pool table to the right. "Drakes there," he nodded, "has come on board to do just that."

Wheeler shifted his gaze across the room. "Why the hell would you bring him in? He's the one who screwed up the whole Miller thing. Hell, he killed the guy, for Christ's sake."

"Precisely. He didn't get paid for that job either. That didn't sit well with him. He's needing some revenge," Slim said.

Wheeler squinted at Drakes. "I don't like bringing him in."

Drakes caught Wheeler's stare and threw his stick on the pool table, and then downed his drink. "I'm through, boys," he said to the men he shot pool with. "Catch you on the down side."

Wheeler watched Drakes's slow, cocky stroll in his direction and his stomach tightened. Nope, this wasn't a good idea at all.

Drakes held out his hand for Wheeler to shake. "Well, well. If it isn't old Deputy Dawg himself. Long time, no see. I wondered when we'd have a run in. I just never figured we'd be on the same side."

Wheeler's cheek twitched at Drakes's grin. Instead of reaching for his hand, he reached for his beer and stared up at him. "If it were up to me, you wouldn't be here. But it seems I wasn't consulted on this important detail," Wheeler said and nodded toward Cowboy.

Cowboy stood and shook Drakes's hand. "Sit down. We have things to discuss."

Slim rested his arms on the table as Drakes sat. "Okay, so here's how the plan is going to go."

Cowboy sat back with a quizzical grin. "Since when're you callin' the play?"

Slim dropped his gaze and mumbled, "Sorry, got excited, is all."

"Little bro thinks he's all grown up cuz we lettin' him in on this," He leaned forward, as did the others. "All right, boys, now this here is how it is. Drakes here is gonna snatch up little Suzie Loo Who and—"

"Who?" Slim asked.

Cowboy closed his eyes. "You idiot, the *kid*."

The light went on behind Slim's eyes. "Oh! Gotcha."

Cowboy continued. "Anyway, Drakes gets the kid and takes her to Cousin Miller's abandoned house."

"Well, the boathouse down by the river, to be more accurate," Slim said.

Cowboy glared at Slim. "You gonna let me tell it? One more crack in and I'll knock you one."

"Sorry," Slim said.

Wheeler rubbed his chin. "I'll be at the station with the sheriff. Cowboy, you and Slim need to be somewhere public. Make a ruckus so people remember you." Wheeler looked at Drakes. "I'm assuming no one knows you're back in town, am I right?"

"Yep. Been quiet as a mouse since I got here."

"Good, at least you've done something right," Wheeler said.

"Now, wait just a—" Drakes started.

Slim put his hand on Drakes's arm. "Now, he didn't mean nothin' by it, did you, Wheeler?"

Wheeler snickered. "Nope, nothing much." He finished his beer and signaled to the waitress for another. "Anyway, that leaves Drakes to babysit until we get our money."

"And the land," Slim said.

"Yeah, and the land," Wheeler said over the rim of his glass.

Drakes let his hand slide over the rump of the waitress as she left their drinks and then licked his lips. "Mmm. Gonna have me some of that."

"In your dreams," Wheeler said. "That look she just gave you? That was disgust, not lust."

"And you're such a pretty boy, are ya?" Drakes asked.

"Prettier than you."

Drakes moved to stand and Slim once again placed a hand on his arm. "We don't need trouble between us. We have to get along, at least through this here job. Too much money at stake to blow it."

Drakes slowly returned to sitting. "Yeah, you're right. But I don't need to put up with his crap." He glared piercingly at Wheeler. "Stay out of my way. You do your job, I'll do mine, and we'll be just fine."

Wheeler chuckled and tipped his beer toward Drakes. "Agreed," he said and took a slow sip. *I have a feeling you'll be dead before the job's done.* He grinned. "Agreed."

CHAPTER TWENTY-THREE

Cassie rushed through her barn chores and finished just after lunch, then returned to the house to find Kate sitting at the kitchen table. "Hey, Mom, I've got some things to do in town," she mumbled.

Kate didn't respond. Instead, she stared down at the letter in her hand.

"Everything okay?" Cassie asked.

Kate looked up, surprised. "Oh, I didn't hear you come in." She stood, confused.

"Mom, are you all right?" Cassie's stomach tightened.

Kate went to the sink and started to do dishes.

Cassie moved to her side and touched her arm. "Mom, you're kind of freaking me out. Is everything okay?"

Kate smiled and sniffled. "I'm sorry, honey. I don't mean to..." She stopped doing dishes and closed her eyes. "No, everything's not all right." She turned toward Cassie. "Roger says we're losing. He's trying his best, but it doesn't seem to be good enough."

"How can we be losing? None of this is even our fault! How can that be? I thought Roger said not to worry." Cassie stared at Kate and shook her head. "This isn't happening. No way is this happening."

"Honey." Kate reached for Cassie but she spun away.

"What are we going to do?" Cassie whispered.

"I know, honey. It'll be okay. You'll see. Everything will work out."

"How can you say that to me? Another lie! Nothing will be okay. Ever!" Cassie yelled and ran from the house. She was in her car and peeling out on the gravel driveway by the time Kate made it to the porch.

Cassie reached for her cell phone and dialed Jess's number.

"Hello?"

"Jess, it's me, Cassie. We need to talk."

"Not really anything to say."

"Yeah, there is. Will you meet me at Grenada Plaza near the GameStop?"

Jess didn't answer.

"Come on, Jess. It's really important. I need your help."

Dead air drifted between them. Jess cleared her throat. "Fine, I'll be there in half an hour."

"I'm on my way, too." Cassie paused. "Thanks."

\###

Cassie arrived at the Plaza first. She pulled into the parking lot by the game store, shut off her car, and waited. Anxiety squeezed at her chest. Her stomach growled and she placed her palm on her belly, then glanced at the clock on the dashboard. 2:15. She dialed Jess once more and told her to meet her inside Gus's.

Cassie pulled the bun off the burger and added ketchup to it, then squeezed a large amount over her fries. She picked one up and bit off the end, staring out the window as a mother chased her young son to her car. A moment later, Jess's tan Nova crossed the lot and parked next to Cassie's car.

The small bells above the door jingled when Jess entered the diner. Cassie waved her to the table.

"Hey," Jess said.

"Hi. Thanks for coming."

Jess glanced down at Cassie's burger and fries and grimaced.

"Want some?"

"Uh, yeah, I don't think so, carnivore."

Cassie shrugged and dipped another already ketchup-soaked fry in more of the same, then leaned her head back like a bird and dropped it in. She reached for her Coke and swallowed. "So anyway. I asked you here because I need your help. You know Larson's after our farm. My mom says it looks like he's going to get it. We have to stop him.

Jess didn't speak.

"C'mon, Jess. You know as well as I do he's a crook...and a murderer. He's even using his own daughter's accident to make a gain."

Jess's head shot up and she glared at Cassie.

Bingo.

Jess softened and she stared down at the table. "I think I overheard something today. Just a little while ago. Mr. Larson and Deputy Wheeler were at my house. Larson was in the study talking with my father, and Wheeler was on his cell phone in my kitchen. I think I heard him telling someone he faked Derrick's Breathalyzer."

"I knew it!"

"Yeah, and I found Deputy Wheeler's accident report. He said Derrick failed the Breathalyzer." Jess continued to stare across the table. "Only thing is, you're right. Derrick wasn't drinking that night."

"We'll have to get that report. You have access to places in the police station that most of us can't get to. You have to get it, or something, anything to paint this any color other than black and white."

Jess shook her head. "No way. I've already got myself in deep enough. If he finds out I lied, my father will send me away for sure. I can't risk that. Besides, I'm not feeling the warm and fuzzies about helping Derrick. Even if he wasn't drunk, he nearly killed Belle. He needs to pay for that."

Cassie squinted at her. "I don't think Derrick should lose his life over this. It was an accident. An accident brought on by you and Belle."

Jess clenched her jaw and stood. "And just how do you intend on proving that without my help?"

Cassie reached for her arm. "Will you just stop and listen for a minute?"

"I know where this is going. He's your boyfriend. If you want to help him, even after what he did to you, then that's your choice. It doesn't mean I have to. Because of him, Belle's lying half dead in the hospital."

"You keep saying that, but is that really the truth? Is it really because of him? Or is this more Belle's fault than anyone else's?"

Jess glared down at her. "Even if it was her fault, she didn't deserve this."

"No, and I didn't deserve any of this, either. That family is destroying us. I mean, what have we done to them? Why are they doing this? What did I ever do that was so bad to Belle to make her want to steal my horse?"

Jess softened slightly. "I'm sorry."

Cassie sat back in her chair. "Then sit and hear me out."

Jess sighed and sat down. "Make it quick."

"The way I see it, Mr. Larson is doing everything possible to make sure Derrick goes to prison for this accident. He's even gotten the courts to agree to try him as an adult."

"Then he needs a good lawyer," Jess said with a smirk.

Cassie sighed and shook her head. "Look, I know you hate him and hold him responsible. But really, how did all this come about? He never invited you two to the farm. That's a lie you made up to cover for Belle. And you were both at Lloyd's party. I know that, too."

Jess rolled her eyes and stared out the window. "Really? You have someone to back that little theory up?" She gave Cassie a snide glare. "Besides, so what if we did go to the party? Derrick did call and asked Belle over. She didn't want to go alone, so she asked me to go with her, and I did." Jess paused. "That's what friends do. They stand by each other."

"You're lying. Derrick would never have called Belle." Cassie's eyes clouded with recollection. "Is that what this is about? Are you trying to get even with me for last summer? For not covering for you?

What was I supposed to do?"

"You could have stood by me and not let me take the rap for stealing those jeans."

"You honestly think I should have said I did it? I mean, really? And have that on my record?"

Jess leaned forward and clenched her jaw. "You were sixteen. And you were squeaky clean. It wouldn't have amounted to anything for you."

"My mom would have—"

"Nothing. She wouldn't have done anything to you. But my father...he's the freaking sheriff! I ended up with community service for the entire summer, and he kept me under lock and key for nearly the whole school year. Nice way to stand by your best friend."

"I told you not to take them, Jess," Cassie reminded her, exasperated. "I was a friend who tried to talk you out of making a bad decision. You had the money. I still don't understand why you did it."

"No, and you never will. You live your peachy little life with your perfect mother on your perfect farm. What would you know about...oh, whatever." Jess focused back on the parking lot. "The answer is no. I'm not going to help you or your bastard boyfriend."

Cassie leaned forward and folded her arms on the table. "Jess, please. This isn't you. I can't believe you'll let so many people suffer just to save your hide. The truth will come out and Derrick will get off. I'm going to see to it."

"Says you. My father has a Breathalyzer. Sounds pretty solid to me."

"Then your father will be making a terrible mistake. One that you and he will have to live with for the rest of your lives. You'll both be liars."

Jess stood and her chair flipped back. "My father is not a liar. He's the sheriff. You're the liar. You'd say anything to save that boyfriend of yours. Even after all he's done. You're pathetic. I bet he could kill your mother and you'd still protect him."

People stopped eating and talking, and stared at both of them.

"Jess, stop, I didn't mean it that way. All I meant was—"

"Yeah, I know what you meant. And you're wrong. You think you have it all figured out. You think you know everything. Well, you don't. In fact, here's a little bit of news I bet you didn't know. I've been called to be a witness in Derrick's trial. And just guess what I'm going to say."

Cassie gasped. "You can't. You'll be lying on stand. That's perjury."

"Wanna bet? He's going to jail. There's no doubt about that." Jess spun away and stormed out.

Cassie watched her get into her car and drive off, and for a moment, just for a moment, she wished her car into a tree.

CHAPTER TWENTY-FOUR

Cassie glanced at the clock above the fireplace and feigned a yawn. 9:15. "Hey, Mom, I'm going to the lower barn and check on the horses before bed. I want to make sure I put the garden rakes away."

"Noah would have done that for you if you hadn't," Kate said.

"Yeah, I know, but I want to check on Dillon. He was limping again."

"Okay, honey. But don't stay out there too long. And take the Taser with you."

"Mom—"

"I mean it. There's all kinds of critters out there this time of night."

Cassie's thoughts went to Derrick and she smirked. "Fine."

###

Derrick stood at the top of the loft, leaning on the railing, waiting for her.

Cassie climbed the ladder. "Hey," she said when she got to the top.

"Hey."

"We need to talk," she said, and moved past him toward the stacks of hay fluffed up the loose hay on the floor and made herself comfortable.

Derrick pulled a wooden chair from the corner of the loft, spun it around, and then straddled it, his arms folded on the back. He rested his chin on his hands and nodded at her. "So…talk."

"I thought you should know something about Jess."

"Yeah, she hates me, too. I already know that."

"Did you know they're going to call her to testify?"

Derrick's lips tightened into thin lines. "No, I didn't. I guess it only makes sense. It is her story that they're mostly going by, anyway, right?"

"Derrick, listen. I talked to her today. She said she's going to stick to her story and that you're going to jail."

Derrick huffed and stood up from the chair. He shoved his hands in his pockets and kicked at the hay. "What did I ever do to her to make her hate me so much? She was there. She knows it was an accident. She knows how this all happened. What's her problem?"

"She admitted to me that you weren't drinking."

Derrick's eyes widened. "That's great!"

"Not exactly. She's not willing to say it on the stand. Seems she has a vendetta against me as well. I'm going to try to get them to let me testify, but it will be her word against mine. There isn't any concrete proof that you weren't drinking," Cassie said, and motioned to the spot beside her.

Derrick sat and stared at his hands. "What's up with her? Why is she doing this?"

"Up until last year, Jess and I had been best friends. Since fifth grade. But when we got into high school, things changed. She started getting into all kinds of trouble and she brought me along for the ride more than once. My schoolwork dropped and I never wanted to help at the barn. My mom and I argued constantly." Cassie chewed on a piece of hay. "Then, last summer, Jess stole a pair of jeans from JCPenney. Because I was with her, they brought us both to the security office and called our parents. Remember, her father is the sheriff. She wanted me to take the fall for it because her father was already on the warpath from her previous issues. I refused to and she got really angry. Her father made her pay for it all summer long, and she was grounded most of the school year. My mom had about had it with all the problems, and said I couldn't hang out with Jess anymore." Cassie scoffed. "She didn't really have to say anything. Jess had already told me to take a hike."

"Yeah, I can see how that would happen."

Cassie shot a hard gaze at him. "What do you mean? You think I should have said I stole the jeans?"

"No, not at all. All I meant was, I can see how, in her way of thinking, that she'd feel that way. She wasn't much of a friend, anyway. If she was, she would've never asked you to do it."

"Yeah, that's what I thought, too." Cassie returned to her seat by Derrick. "Anyway, then Belinda moved to town. Her family's so rich and her father's so powerful that I think Jess saw a perfect opportunity to get a free ride. Not that her family is poor or anything, just that with Belinda she'd have more of everything. And she did. Mr. Larson likes having the sheriff as a friend. The sheriff has looked the other way on a couple of occasions where Belle was concerned, but he's not crooked. Cassie shifted and faced Derrick. "That is, until this. The accident is way too big for the sheriff to simply look the other way. So Larson did the next best thing. He attacked me and my mother and became rabid as a raccoon in daylight for you. This way he makes out fat. He gets our farm, has you put in jail, and takes the heat off Belle."

Derrick stood and looked down at her. "You've really got this all figured out, huh?"

"Sort of. It makes sense, doesn't it?"

"Yeah, I suppose."

Cassie rose to her feet. "I have a plan. I'll talk to Jess once more. I think I can get her to see what she's doing is totally wrong. I think I can get her to at least get us a copy of the report," Cassie said as she stepped down onto the ladder through the hole in the floor. "I'll call you if I get anything." She paused, eying him quizzically. "Hey, you all right? What're you thinking?"

"I'm thinking it's time for me to take things into my own hands," he replied, his voice hard. "This is my life we're talking about. Not that I don't appreciate what you're doing to help me, but—"

"What's that supposed to mean?"

Derrick glared at her. "Just what I said."

"And what do you think you're going to do?"

"What no one else seems to be able to. I'm going to get to the truth, one way or another."

"I think you should just leave it to me. You'll just complicate things more."

Derrick sneered. "Complicate things more? Really? How much

more complicated do you think I can make this? No, Cassie. I appreciate your help, but I need to take things into my own hands. I at least have to try."

Cassie stood on the ladder, her head and shoulders showing above the floor. "I'll come by tomorrow and we can talk about it then. I'm doing everything I can to help you. Just don't do anything stupid between now and then. You hear me? Wait for me."

Derrick scoffed and shuffled in the hay. "I need to talk to Jess face-to-face. I have to make her tell the truth."

"As you said, she hates you. She'll never talk to you. And if she sees you, she may hate you even more. I think it would be a mistake."

Derrick stared at Cassie through squinted eyes. "It'll be a mistake, all right. Hers."

CHAPTER TWENTY-FIVE

On the drive back to the hospital for her afternoon visit with Belle, Cassie's words hung in the air and echoed in Jess's ears. *None of us deserved any of this. If it wasn't for Belle, this wouldn't be happening. Derrick is going to be tried as an adult. His life will be ruined. My mother says we're going to lose the fight against Frank Larson. We'll lose everything.*

Jess slipped into the darkened room and frowned. She walked across to the window and pulled the heavy drapes back, exposing the late afternoon sunlight. "Why your mother thinks you need to live in total darkness just because you're in a coma really pisses me off." She put her purse down on the shelf and took up her usual spot in the green chair beside Belle's bed. "So, you sleeping or are you awake?"

I'm awake now, thank you very much.

"It doesn't matter. I'll just talk to you as if you were awake. Okay? I have a lot on my mind and if I don't get it out, I'm going to explode."

Sure, why not. Not like I'm doing much anyway. Why don't you just tell me everything that's on your little mind? It doesn't matter that I'm stuck here with thoughts of my own that I can't get out. It doesn't matter that I'm going crazy trapped inside this alternate world of—

"Okay, so here it is. You know how I said that I wanted Derrick to pay for what he did to you? Well, that is true, but I've been thinking. Maybe juvie won't be so bad."

No way. My father would never let that happen.

"I mean, I don't know why I didn't just tell the truth to begin with. I've never been one to run away from things." She pulled the TV controller from the nightstand and wrapped the cord around the bed railing. "When Deputy Wheeler showed up at the accident and I told him what had happened, and he asked me if I was sure that that's how it all happened, I guess I just panicked. Then when he walked over to Derrick and told him he smelled like a brewery I thought of this whole scheme to get myself off the hook. So, I made up this story that Derrick had gotten drunk at Lloyd's party and then invited you and me to the farm. Deputy Wheeler backed up my story to my father and he believed me, too."

So, you hung Derrick out to dry. Nice going. I'm proud of you. He deserves to pay for this.

"I wanted to tell the truth, really, but then my father turned up stuff from Derrick's past that made him look even more guilty. Remember I said he was involved in a prior accident? Everything just seemed to be falling in place for me. I was out clean, and Derrick would pay for what he did to you. But now..." Jess reached out and took Belle's hand. "God, Belle, I don't know what to do."

What don't you know? Stick to the plan. Keep your mouth shut and let Derrick pay.

"I've done a lot of things wrong and gotten in a lot of trouble, but it was always harmless. No one ever got hurt because of it. I mean, not really. I caused some trouble in school, stole some small stuff and did minor property damage—I even drove without a license. But this is different."

He's the one who got into an accident and killed someone. Obviously he can't drive. He's a menace and needs to be off the streets. Never mind what he's done to me. What are we talking? A few months in juvenile detention? Big deal. Look at me!

"He could go away for a long time. Cassie said that your father has gotten the courts to try him as an adult. That's really bad. That means he'll go to adult prison instead of juvenile detention."

My father?

"It'll ruin Derrick's life. And his family's life. At first, I didn't think they'd be able to make the charges stick. I thought that Derrick would just go through the trial process and then get off. You know, I wanted him to be afraid, to squirm. But this. This is *not* what I'd planned."

Wait, I don't understand. Why would my father do all this?

"They have evidence now, too. But the thing is, it's fake. Falsified. I heard Deputy Wheeler telling someone on the phone that he was able to fake it. And I heard your father say they have a Breathalyzer on Derrick that proves he was over the legal limit. How can that be? Derrick never even had a drink that night. We both know that."

Jess stood and walked around the bed to the table with the pitcher of water and poured herself a cup. She took a long sip, then squeezed the plastic cup and tossed it in the trash. "Cassie knows I'm lying, but she can't prove it. She's smart, though. She'll figure it out before long." Jess walked to the foot of the bed and glanced down at Belle. "Tell you the truth, I'm not the least bit surprised that she's forgiven Derrick and is trying to help him, even after he killed her horse. That's the way she is."

Oh my God! Arco's dead? I killed him?

"I think that even after what you did, she'd even forgive you. She's always saying that it's not our place to judge, and that there's only one real judge and jury, and that's God." She continued to her chair and sat down. The television remote hung loosely over the bed rail and Jess picked it up, aiming it at the TV. The news came on without the volume. She gazed down at Belle. "A part of me feels very sorry for her, too. From what Cassie says, your father has managed to get the Grain and Feed Shop to stop selling them their horse feed. They're close to losing the farm."

He's taking their farm? And their home? Why would he do that?

"If you ask me, I think your father used this accident to get the Rhyne's property. Everyone knows he's been trying to for a long time."

What are you saying? That he used me as an excuse? That he used me? He may be cold-hearted when it comes to business, but he'd never go so low as to use his own daughter. You're sick! Get out. I want you out of my room. GET OUT!

"Anyway, this whole thing has gotten so out of control. I wouldn't even be surprised if it was your father who convinced Deputy Wheeler to falsify the Breathalyzer."

Are you crazy? How about your father, the almighty sheriff? Maybe it was him!

Jess stood, moved to the window, and stared out at the darkening sky. "We've got about another half hour of sunlight. Can you tell that? I wonder what it's like for you in there."

Get out of my room! Nurse! I want you out, and don't come back!

Jess walked back to the bed and smiled down at Belle. "Okay, honey," she said, and held Belle's hand in hers. She brought it to her lips and kissed it lightly. "I'm going to run for now. Don't worry about anything I've told you. I'm just glad you were here to listen."

Get out! I hate you.

"I'll figure this out. I'm supposed to testify. I'm thinking I'll tell the truth. You're in a coma, so it's not like they can do anything to you. Me? Well, I need to own up to my own mistakes. I can't let Derrick take this much of a fall. And if Wheeler and your father really did mess with legal documents, then they deserve to be punished too." Jess set Belle's hand gently on the bed and walked to the door. "Thanks for listening." She gave a light laugh. "Even in a coma you manage to help me."

Don't you dare come back here! How could you say those things about my father? I hate you!

Jess blew Belle a kiss. "I love you. See you tomorrow. I'll tell you all about court."

CHAPTER TWENTY-SIX

Cassie rubbed her eyes and opened them to the banging at her bedroom door.

"Cassie, wake up," Kate called.

"Mom, what's wrong?" Cassie asked as she slithered out of bed. She stumbled to the door and pulled it open.

Kate rushed in around her and stood in the middle of the room. She wrapped her thin sweater tighter around her body and shifted on her feet. "Come here, sweetheart. Sit down."

Cassie stepped toward her mother. "Mom, what is it? You're scaring me."

"Where were you last night before you came home?"

"Why?"

"Just tell me."

"I stopped by the mall, then drove by Nancy's, but she wasn't home so I came home. I didn't want to come in right away, so I went up Willow Tree Lane to the brook to think. Why? What's going on?"

Kate walked to the window. Again, she pulled her arms tighter around her body. "He's gone. Apparently, he ran away from home."

Cassie sat at the corner of her bed. "What do you mean? Why would he do that?" she asked hoping her mother wouldn't see through her lies.

Kate sat on the bed beside her. "The police are on their way here. They want to question you."

Cassie stared at Kate. "He didn't tell me anything about leaving."

"Are you sure you don't know where he is? You're not hiding him?"

"Mom, I—"

Kate stood and looked down at Cassie, and then gave her a nervous smile. "Okay, honey. Then we have nothing to worry about." Kate kissed the top of Cassie's head. "You should get dressed. The deputy will be here any minute." She walked to the door and glanced back before leaving. Again, she smiled weakly before disappearing down the hall.

Cassie walked to the window and looked out toward the lane and guilt squeezed at her stomach. She didn't really lie. She was going to tell the truth. It's not her fault her mother jumped to the conclusion that she was going to say no, she wasn't hiding Derrick. Still, guilt clawed inside her. "I hope you know what you're doing, Derrick," she mumbled.

She dressed quickly and went downstairs. Kate had already gone out to the barn. She'd prepared a small breakfast of eggs and toast for Cassie before she left, but Cassie's stomach was too tense to eat. She went to the refrigerator and took out the orange juice, poured a glass, took a sip, and dumped the rest down the sink.

Muffled voices drifted through the kitchen window. Cassie leaned over the sink and peered outside and noticed the tail end of the sheriff's car parked past the oak tree by the porch. Kate's powder blue sweater peeked through the gray moss-covered branches. A moment later, the front door opened and Kate entered the house.

"Cassie?"

"I'm in the kitchen."

"Deputy Wheeler is here," Kate called. "He'd like to talk to you."

Cassie placed a smile on her face and stepped out into the living room.

Deputy Wheeler sprawled out across the sofa and smiled as she entered. "Hey, Cassie." He grinned. "Come sit over by me, here. I have a few questions I was hoping you could help answer for me."

Cassie remained standing under the arched doorway, her arms crossed in front of her. "About what?"

"As you know, Derrick's on the run. His folks said other than themselves, you were probably the last one who saw him. Said you paid him a visit a couple of nights ago?"

"I was there, yeah. He said he was going to bed after I left."

"Mind if I ask what you talked about?"

Kate moved toward Cassie. "Deputy Wheeler, would you like some coffee?"

Wheeler flashed a broad smile. "Sure, Kate. That sounds great. Thank you."

Kate and Cassie exchanged a glance as Kate brushed past. Cassie gazed at Wheeler. "We didn't say much. His trial starts soon. I wanted to try to comfort him and let him know I'd be there for him. Stuff like that."

"Hmm. I thought you guys were on the outs. According to Jess, you broke up with him. Not that anyone would blame you. I mean, he did kill your horse and cheat on you."

Cassie glared at him through narrowed eyes. She clenched her jaw to contain her voice. "He didn't kill my horse. That spoiled rotten princess killed my horse. And I don't care what Jess said, he did not and would not ever cheat on me with Belinda Larson."

Wheeler averted his eyes to the coffee table and laughed softly. "Um, yeah. Never with the likes of a beautiful rich girl. I see your point." Before Cassie could rebut, he continued, "Did he mention anything about leaving home?"

"No."

Wheeler stood and picked up his deputy's hat. He moved toward Cassie, stopped in front of her, and gazed down. He spun his hat around his fingers and squinted. His voice lowered to a menacing tone. "Did he mention anything about Jess?"

Cassie bent back slightly to gain some distance from his hovering torso. "Deputy Wheeler, we've been down this road before. You've already questioned me about all this. Nothing's changed."

Wheeler leaned even closer. "Oh, I'd say a lot has changed. It seems Jess Winslow is missing now, and folks place you and her at Gus's diner sometime late afternoon yesterday."

Cassie's eyes widened. "What do you mean missing?"

"You know, missing, as in she never returned home last night. Seems a little funny, don't you think? I mean, that she should happen to go missing while this boy is on the run? As far as we can tell, she made her afternoon visit to the hospital to see Belle, and that was the last time anyone saw her." He watched Cassie with careful eyes.

"I had lunch with her at the diner around 2:00, that's true."

"Then it would seem you were one of the last ones to see her, too," he said, spinning his hat again. "What did you girls talk about?"

"Not much. Belle, the trial, and she said she was still angry with me because of last summer. She got in trouble with her father because I wouldn't lie for her. We're not exactly friends anymore because of it."

Wheeler chuckled. "Yeah, that was a doozy of a time for the sheriff. He didn't know whether to lock her up in her room or put her in a jail cell. She really tried that man's patience."

Cassie didn't smile. "Is there anything else?"

Wheeler's face hardened. "Yeah, I want to know where your boyfriend is and what he knows about Jess Winslow."

"What are you saying? You think Derrick had something to do with Jess not coming home?"

Wheeler smirked. "Crossed my mind. Or maybe you? You just admitted you two ain't no longer friends."

Cassie moved around him into the living room.

The smirk never left his face. Confident? Cocky? Arrogant? She couldn't place it. All she knew was that this man she once trusted now made her skin crawl. Before she knew what she was saying, words blurted from her mouth. "For all we know, *you* did something with her. Maybe you kidnapped her."

Wheeler's smile disappeared for the briefest of moments. "Me? Why would I want Jess to disappear? She's the sheriff's daughter.

She's like my little sister."

"Precisely. And you're his deputy. A crooked one, at that. And you don't exactly seem broken up about her being missing."

Wheeler walked to her and stared hard into her eyes. "And just why would you call me crooked? You think you know something about me?"

Kate walked in with a tray of coffee and cups and placed it on the coffee table. She poured a cup and held it out to Deputy Wheeler.

Cassie's skin pricked on the back of her neck as he stared and a soft murmur touched her ear.

Careful stepping.

"No. Sorry. I guess you're just making me feel defensive. I'm a kid. It was a stupid remark."

Wheeler continued to glare, but then the grin returned. "Yeah, well, I guess all kids act stupid now and again." He placed his hat on his head and walked to the door, ignoring the outstretched coffee cup. He opened the door and looked back. "I'll be in touch," he said with a nod, and then he was gone. His footsteps echoed off the wooden porch as he walked away, whistling.

CHAPTER TWENTY-SEVEN

Cassie briefed her mother on their conversation after Deputy Wheeler left.

"That boy certainly isn't turning out to be who I thought he was," Kate said.

Cassie looked at her wide-eyed. "Mom you can't be serious. You believe that Derrick has something to do with Jess going missing? That's crazy."

"Come on, Cassie. It isn't looking very good for him."

"Exactly. Don't you think Mr. Larson has planned it out perfectly?"

Now Kate stared bug-eyed. "Larson? Oh, Cassie." She sighed, rubbing her temples. "Honey, this really is getting out of hand. Now you're accusing this man of kidnapping?"

"Really? Look what he's done lately. He doesn't even seem to care about Belle. He hardly ever visits her. All he cares about is our property, and the Miller place. He wants to build an empire and I don't think anything is beneath him. I mean anything."

Kate furrowed her brows, sat on the sofa, and sipped at the coffee she'd prepared for Deputy Wheeler. She gently lowered the cup and saucer to the coffee table and folded her hands on her lap. "You know, for a young girl, sometimes you sound like you have more sense than half the town put together." Kate stood and walked toward the kitchen doorway. "I'm going to call Roger."

"Great. I'm going out to the barn to start feeding," Cassie said and rushed for the door. She jumped from the porch and ran toward the barn. Just when she started to believe in him again. Now this?

She slid the barn door open and saw Noah standing at the end with the wheel barrow and a pitchfork. *Well, this sucks.* She moved down the aisle, glancing into a couple of the stalls as she did. "Hey, Noah. Sorry I'm late."

"No problem. I see you and your mom had a visitor."

"Oh, you saw that? Yeah, Deputy Wheeler stopped by to tell us something terrible has happened. It seems that Jessica Winslow has disappeared. She never made it home yesterday after she left the hospital."

Noah's eyebrows lifted. "Is that so?" He shook his head and tsked. "That's unfortunate. Sure she'll turn up, though. Prob'ly just wandering around, thinkin' and such."

"Yeah, you're probably right." Cassie smiled. She climbed the ladder to the loft up to her shoulders and glanced inside. Derrick wasn't there. "I was going to start on the stalls," she said absently.

"Got that covered. You just go do somethin' fun."

Cassie frowned and looked down at him.

"Well, go do somethin' other than work around here. I'll take care of things. I'm a bit ahead of my schedule anyhow."

Cassie climbed down the ladder, went to him, and kissed his cheek. "Noah, you're the best. As a matter of fact, I do have some things that I really need to get done. Thanks."

"My pleasure, miss," Noah smiled and nodded.

###

Cassie drove for several hours, up and down nearly every street, looking for Derrick or Jess, dreading finding them almost as much as she dreaded not finding them. "Where are you guys?" she said to the air. She phoned Derrick's cell for the fifth time, and again no answer. Cursing, she tossed the phone on the seat beside her. A moment later, Katy Perry's *Alien* music played from beneath her purse. She reached under and grabbed her phone, then slid the bar across the screen to unlock it. "Hello? Hello!"

"Cass, it's me."

"God, Derrick! Where are you? Why haven't you answered any of my calls?"

"I got rid of my cell phone in case they put a tracker on it. I'm at a pay phone just outside of Beaumont."

"How'd you get all the way there?"

"I hitchhiked."

Cassie pulled the car over and parked beneath an old oak tree. "Jeez, Derrick, I thought we agreed you wouldn't do anything stupid. The police are looking for you."

Derrick chuckled. "Uh, yeah, duh."

"Did you really do something to Jess?"

"What do you mean?"

"Jess is missing. They think you had something to do with it." Cassie paused for a split second. "So, did you?"

"No! What do you mean, she's missing?"

"Deputy Wheeler was at my house questioning me this morning about it. I swear, Derrick, if you've done anything to her—"

"Oh, for...you have to be kidding me. You don't seriously think I had anything to do with it."

Cassie didn't respond.

"Are you crazy?"

"I'm sorry. But you did say you were going to take things into your own hands, and she *was* scheduled to testify! What am I supposed to think?"

"Not that I had anything to do with it, for one. I can't believe you. Ever think I'm being framed?"

"How could you be framed if no one knew you were planning on running?"

"I don't know. All I know is I didn't do it."

Cassie looked in her rear view mirror as a police car approached. "Where are you, exactly? I'll come pick you up."

"If they find us before they find her, you'll be an accomplice. No."

"Don't be so stupid! Let me help you. We'd be better off trying to figure this out together. Don't you think?" She watched as the police car crawled past.

Derrick didn't answer.

"By the way. I think I pissed off Deputy Wheeler."

"How?"

"I called him crooked."

"And that pissed him off? Everyone thinks he's crooked."

"Yeah, but when I said it, he really seemed to get angry. He asked me if I thought I knew something about him."

"Do you?"

"Just what I told you. You know, about the Breathalyzer and stuff."

"Cass, stay away from him," Derrick warned. "You could be in danger."

"Then I need you here to protect me. So, where are you?"

"Fine." He sighed. "I'm at Gertrude's Country Store on Main and Connors. You know it?"

"Yeah. I know a shortcut through Old Mill Road. I'll be there in about an hour and a half."

Cassie ended the call and dropped the phone on the passenger seat. She looked around carefully. Butterflies rattled in her stomach and her heart raced. She gripped the steering wheel with her left hand and shifted the car into drive. As she pulled away from the curb, she realized she was holding her breath. "Really, girl. You better get a grip," she scolded herself.

She headed out of town and turned on Old Mill Road, which cut through the Miller place, shortening her trip to I-49 by fifteen minutes. The dirt road was straight and level with a few bumps or holes, making the ride smooth and quick. The bright afternoon sun shone through the tall oak trees and spread a golden glow across the cow pasture. Cassie pulled her visor down and caught a sparkle in the dust in her rear view mirror. A moment later, a car sped up behind her and bumped the rear of her vehicle. She swerved left, then right, before straightening out.

"What the hell?"

The gray car with tinted windows sped up beside her, and Cassie accelerated.

"What is wrong with you? Are you trying to kill someone?" Her adrenaline rose off the charts, and her chest tightened. *I'm going to have a freaking heart attack.*

The gray car rammed its nose into the left side of Cassie's car, forcing her to lose control. She sped off the side of the road through the barbed wire fence, taking down several of the wooden posts. She screamed only once before slamming head on into a tall oak tree.

CHAPTER TWENTY-EIGHT

Cassie, you must wake.

Cassie woke with a start in a sitting position with her back against a wall and tried to focus against the darkness of her blindfold. The early evening sounds echoed through a small open window and the wind carried with it the rich, strong, earthy scent of the swamp. She attempted to stand and noticed her feet were bound. Her head ached. Her thoughts raged. She yanked on her restraints and the pipe clanked against the metal cuffs. She gasped.

"Who's there?" A small, shaky voice called from the shadows.

Cassie trembled and turned her head toward the familiar voice. "It's me. I mean, it's Cassandra Rhyne. Jess? Is that you?"

"Yeah, Cassie! Oh my God. What are you doing here?"

"I don't know. Someone ran me off the road this afternoon. Where are we?"

"I don't know."

"Do you know how you got here?"

"Someone hit me in the head yesterday afternoon when I was leaving the hospital after visiting Belle. Next thing I knew, I was tied up in this dump. There's two of them."

"Two of who?"

"The morons that took us. And they have guns."

Cassie tried to shift her position. "I can't see anything. Where did they go?"

"I don't know. They left about an hour ago. One of them said he was scared you were going to die. You've been unconscious for, like, hours."

"Did you get a look at them?"

"No, I've been blindfolded since I woke up."

Cassie gnawed on her lower lip. "I'm blindfolded too. Okay, did they say anything? Anything at all that would lead you to guess who they are? Or why they took you?"

"No. All one of them said was, 'He'd better pay us for this gig or he's just as dead as she is' and the other guy hit him and told him to shut up. My God, Cass, they're going to kill us. I'm so scared."

Footsteps fell on the wooden steps outside. Cassie's heart pounded in her chest and bile puckered her glands. The door opened and two men stepped inside.

"We shouldn't a brought the other one here. We shoulda kept 'em separated," one of them mumbled with an easy southern drawl.

"That's not how I work," the other said in a thick Creole accent. It's better that we have 'em together. Keeps it cleaner that way."

The sound of heavy boots fell heavily across the creaky wooden floor. There was a small scratch sound and then a soft glow glimmered beneath her blindfold. Again the sound of boots echoed in her ears and a chair skidded on the floor, followed by a heavy object being set down on a table or a counter.

"Why do you keep cleaning that thing?" Southern Accent asked. "You're not gonna be shootin' anythin'."

"This here's 'ole Gladys. And ya just never knows," Creole said. "Heard there's good huntin' in these parts."

"You don't mean—" Southern Accent said.

Creole chuckled. "Like I said, ya never knows."

Both girls whimpered.

"What do you mean hunting, you sick bastards?" Jess called out.

"Shut your mouth. You don't speak unless I say," Creole said. The chair shuffled and a loud crack broke the air, followed by Jess's cries.

"Stop it! You leave her alone, or I swear I'll—" Cassie screamed.

"You'll what? What do you think you're gonna do about it?" Creole moved in front of her. His putrid breath assaulted Cassie's senses as his fingers played with her hair. "You're a pretty one, ya are." He let his hand glide down her neck, over her shoulder, and down her arm. "Yeah, we gonna have some fun, you and me."

"Don't touch me. You smell like a rotting pig," Cassie said.

"Leave her alone, Drakes," Southern Accent said.

"Oh, now see there, Slim? You've gone ahead and used my name." Drakes brushed against Cassie's thigh. "How about if I call out your real name, Slim?"

"No, don't," Southern Accent said.

"Yeah, that's right. 'Cuz you done know these girls. Wouldn't be right they know who ya are. But you went and told them my name.

Seems ya leavin' me no choice but to put 'ole Gladys to work." Drakes snickered. "Isn't that right...Hank?"

"Hank? Is that you? What are you doing?"

In a swift motion, the blindfold lifted from Cassie's eyes. She squinted to focus in the candlelit room and then set her eyes on the rough, rugged man with the scraggly, thick beard kneeling in front of her.

"There. That's better, ain't it?" he said. "Seeing's how you know our names, ain't no reason to keep those pretty eyes hid no more."

Hank rounded the wooden table toward Drakes. "What you doin'? They weren't 'sposed to know."

"'Ain't my doin'. You the one opened ya big mouth. I'm just makin' 'em more comf'table." Drakes shuffled over to Jess and removed her blindfold. "See now, ain't that more comf'table?"

"Oh my God," Jess sobbed. "Please, just let us go. We won't say anything. I promise."

"You know how many times those same words been spoke to me? That's just desperate talkin'. Minute you go free your jaw starts yappin'."

"No! I swear to you. We won't talk. Will we, Cass?"

Cassie stared at Hank. He shuffled his feet side-to-side and gazed at the floor. She turned to Jess without speaking. Jess's eyes widened and her sobs grew.

Drakes stood and sat down at the table. "Let me finish this here sandwich, and then we can begin."

"Begin what?" Hank asked.

"The hunt," Drakes said.

A few minutes later, Drakes pushed away from the table, stood, and stepped to Jess. He leaned down and untied her hands and feet. "Okay, now give us a good run." He lifted her to her feet. "Go!" he yelled.

"I don't understand…" Jess choked.

"I said, go!" he repeated, and shoved her toward the door. "Run. Now."

Jess flung the door open and ran from the shack.

Drakes picked up the shotgun from the table and moved toward the door.

Hank stepped in front of him. "No, I can't let ya' do this. You can't hunt 'em like animals. Besides, we gotta keep her alive. Wheeler won't pay for no dead girl."

"Yeah, well Wheeler ain't payin' me," Drakes grinned. "I got me a new boss man, willing to pay me all of what Wheeler was and then some."

Hank stared in disbelief.

"Move, boy, or I'll shoot ya where ya stand," Drakes said and pushed past him. "You stay here and keep an eye on that one." He stopped in the open doorway and glared at Hank. "And you both better be here when I get back."

Bile crept up the back of Cassie's throat. "You can't be serious! She's a human being. You can't get away with this!"

Drakes scoffed. "You wouldn't think so, would ya? But I been doin' this a long time, and it just gets more and more fun each time. It won't be long. I'm good," he said, winked, and then left.

Cassie's mind went numb with fear, her skin crawled, and her

MISTS OF BAYOU RHYNE

mouth dried. Thoughts flew threw her head in fragments. "Oh my God! Oh my God!"

"I don't think there's no God here, Miss Cassie," Hank said apologetically.

Cassie gazed frantically out the window. "Spirits of the mist, please protect Jess," she chanted over and over. "Please protect Jess."

Hank toyed with his hands, his eyes wide and his lips tight, but he didn't move. "You witchin'?"

Cassie thrashed about, kicking her feet and yanking against the pipe. *"Yes.* And if you don't help, I'm going to tell the spirits of the mist to kill you! Now, go out there and stop him! You can't let him do this!"

A loud noise clanged through the window and Hank jumped. "What was that?!" He walked out onto the porch and stared as the soft mist swirled against the still night air. Then another noise rang out further away.

"Hank, over here!" Drakes yelled. "We got company."

"Crap!" Hank mumbled. "Don't move. I'll be back."

The sounds of Hank's footsteps echoed as they trailed down the steps of the porch, and his voice called out in the distance for Drakes. Another sound, softer, quieter, crept on the creaky planks, and then a silhouette stood in the doorway. Cassie squirmed against the wall and tried desperately to hide in the shadows. The spirits had come to her.

The silhouette moved further inside and the heavy thudding in her chest stopped.

"Cassie? Are you in here?"

His words were like electricity to her heart, restarting it with their sound.

"Oh my God! Derrick, is that you?"

CHAPTER TWENTY-NINE

Frank Larson sat in the green faux leather chair by the hospital bed with Belle's hand resting between his two. Deputy Wheeler stood on the opposite side leaning against the wall strumming his fingers on his leg.

"So, Wheeler, I'm assuming that you've dotted your I's and crossed your T's with this little plan of ours. You're sure the Breathalyzer is foolproof, right? I don't want any mistakes in that courtroom."

Wheeler smirked. "It's solid. You don't have to worry. It doesn't matter what the kid says. I've done this once before and it worked like a charm."

"You better be right."

Wheeler moved toward the door. "Hey, I'm going down to Leroy's for some real coffee. Want me to bring you back one?"

Frank watched Belle's still form and nodded. "That'd be good."

Wheeler's cell phone rang and he pulled it out and read the screen, and then glanced over at Frank.

Frank never took his eyes from Belle.

Wheeler left the room. "What the hell are you calling me for? I told you never to call me." He huffed. "Don't say anything. Let me get to my car and I'll call you back," he said and disconnected without a response. He walked out the glass front doors of the hospital into the soft, misty night air and headed for his cruiser. He pulled his cell phone from his pocket, pressed in Hank's number, and then slid behind the wheel.

"We have a problem," Hank said.

"What?"

"There's, like, there's someone else out here. And I can't control Drakes. He says he ain't workin' for you no more. He's decided to go on a hunting spree with Jess Winslow."

Wheeler's heart thudded in his chest. "What the hell you mean, a hunting spree?"

"I mean, he let her go so he could…you know…hunt her. Then he yelled for me that someone else was in the marsh."

"You freaking idiots. All you were supposed to do was keep her until after the trial. Where is she now?"

"Don't know."

Wheeler pulled out of the lot and headed down Main Street. *"You don't know?"* His throat dried and he ran his fingers through his hair. He pulled up to a red light and stared out at the glistening streets. The light changed, but he didn't move until the car behind him beeped. "He's sold us out."

"What do you mean?"

"What do you think I mean? Larson and Drakes are working together…against us. You get it now?"

Hank cleared his throat. "There's something else."

"What more could go wrong?"

"We have Cassie Rhyne."

"What?!"

"And Drakes took off their blindfolds. They've seen our faces. They know who I am."

"No, no, this isn't happening," Wheeler moaned, pounding the wheel. "Why would he do that?"

"Because I said his name by mistake."

Wheeler drove into the K-Mart parking lot and pulled around back to the receiving area. "I have to think. Where's Drakes now?"

"He had me call Georgie and they're out looking for Jess. He told me to go back to the boathouse to make sure Cassie is okay."

"You left her alone? You've got to be kidding me."

"I had to."

"Uh, one other thing. She was witchin' when I left her. She was talkin' to the spirits of the mist. I heard her say it. She was askin' 'em to help her 'scape."

"That's just great." Wheeler rested his head back and inhaled deeply. "Find them," he demanded and hung up. He sat there for several minutes wondering how everything had gone so wrong. He knew he should have trusted his gut. Drakes has always been bad news. You couldn't trust him. Now he had to fix things. Several plans played through his mind as he drove to Leroy's for the coffees, none of them good ones.

Wheeler walked into Belle's room and glanced at Frank Larson, trying to hide his loathing.

"Everything okay?" Frank asked.

Wheeler nodded. "Just as we planned," he said and held out Frank's coffee.

"Good. No mistakes." Frank stood. "I need to use the head. I'll be back in a few."

Wheeler turned to Belle with a smile. "Things ain't quite as they were planned, but we're gonna fix that. Your little friends have become quite a problem, but not for long." His fingers brushed Belle's cheek. "New plan. It'll look like Derrick Anderson kidnapped both Jess and Cassie. He lured them to the Miller place. Hank was out night hunting gators when he heard some noise coming from the boathouse there." Wheeler wiped at his chin. "Yeah, that's right. He heard some noise, and when he drove his boat over there he saw Anderson with the girls. He says Anderson had already killed the girls, and he pulled a gun when he saw Hank. Hank had no choice but to shoot—self-defense." Wheeler ran his fingers through his hair. "But what about Drakes?" he mumbled.

Frank returned and stood beside Belle's bed opposite Deputy Wheeler.

Wheeler's police mic made a static sound. He pinched the side of the mic. "Deputy Wheeler here."

"This is dispatch. Sheriff Winslow wants you back at the station immediately. We found the Rhyne girl's car down on Old Miller Road."

"She okay?" Wheeler asked.

"Don't know. She wasn't in it," the dispatcher said.

"I'm on my way."

Frank glared up at Wheeler. "The Rhyne girl is missing now?"

"Appears that way," Wheeler said as he shuffled toward the door.
"You wouldn't know anything about that now, would you Frank?"

Frank stared hard but didn't' answer.

"Just figured I'd ask. I'll let you know what I find out."

Daddy, what are you doing? What's happened to Cassie?

Frank nodded, reached for Belle's hand, and smiled. "Ah, Belle,
everything is working out just fine." He set her hand down on the bed
and stood. He leaned both arms on the bed railing and smiled down at
her. "No reason to let this unfortunate accident of yours be for nothing.
Soon, I'll have all of the Rhyne and Miller properties and then I'll own
more than two thirds of this town. Know what that means? I'll have
succeeded in literally owning my own town." He patted her hand.
"Thank you darlin'."

*Daddy, no! You can't do this. Do you even know what the deputy is
planning? Please! Oh, God, I have to wake up. Please!*

"I'll stop in again soon, sweetheart."

###

After Wheeler and Frank Larson parted ways at the hospital
parking garage, Wheeler headed east toward the police station. He
pulled into the station lot and entered the building. Sheriff Winslow
was sitting on the corner of Sheppard's desk, leaning forward in
conversation. They both looked up as he entered.

"Wheeler, in my office. You, too, Sheppard," Sheriff Winslow
said.

Wheeler glanced at Sheppard and then they followed the sheriff into the small office at the corner of the room.

"Sit down," Sheriff Winslow said pointing to the two wooden chairs in front of his desk. He sat and pulled out a folder. "I just received a phone call from Katherine Rhyne. Seems we have our third Missing Persons in less than forty-eight hours. I want these kids found, and I want them found alive. I don't know what's going on here, but—"

"Excuse me, Sheriff, but how long has Cassie been missing? It's only seven o'clock. Missing dinner shouldn't be cause for alarm," Wheeler said.

Sheriff Winslow set a hard stare on Wheeler. "It's not that she missed dinner. It's that we found her car nose deep against an oak tree on Old Miller Road. The driver's side was pretty much dented and scraped from the rear on up. Looks like someone sideswiped her into the tree."

"What do you want us to do, Sheriff?" Sheppard asked.

"I want you boys out on the streets asking questions. I called in George Marrow and Lee Thompson. They're covering the boatyards along the corridor." Sheriff Winslow stared down at his desk with pursed lips.

Wheeler stood. "Right, that means they'll have most of the north and east side of town covered." He turned toward Sheppard. "I'll take the west side, you take the south. We can cover more ground that way." *And while I'm at it, I'll just head on down to the Miller place and straighten out a little mess going on there.*

Mary Turner, the dispatcher, appeared in the doorway. "Sorry to bother you, sir, but I just received a call from Old Lady Braxton. She seems to think she just saw the girls—Cassandra Rhyne and your daughter—crossing over by the railroad tracks behind her house." She walked forward and handed the sheriff a sticky note with a scribbled address and then left the room.

Deputy Sheppard smirked. "Old Lady Braxton has a habit of seeing things. How many times a week does she call about someone on the railroad tracks, only for us to find that there was never anyone there? She calls when she's lonely. I doubt she saw the girls."

"Maybe so," Sheriff Winslow said, "but it's possible. Wheeler and I will—"

A soft knock sounded at the door and Mary appeared once again. "Sir, there's been reports of shots fired out around Bayou Rhyne by the Miller place. Would you like me to send Deputies Marrow and Thompson out there?"

Wheeler's stomach tightened and he clenched his jaw. "It's probably the Hickman brothers out gator hunting," he said. "They live out there by the Miller place. I'll check it out."

Mary backed out and silently shut the door.

Sheriff Winslow rose to his feet and placed his Sheriff's baseball cap on his head. He handed the sticky note to Sheppard. "Sheppard, you check out Mrs. Braxton's report. Wheeler and I will head out to the Miller place. Let me know as soon as you know anything."

"Yes, sir." Sheppard nodded, took the sticky note, and left the office.

Wheeler cleared his throat. "Sir, if you want to go with Sheppard, that's fine. I can handle the other call myself."

Sheriff Winslow cast Wheeler a sideways look. "You minding me coming along with you to Bayou Rhyne?"

Wheeler shifted on his feet. "No, sir."

Winslow continued to stare at Wheeler a moment longer. "Good. Let's move out."

Wheeler followed the sheriff out of the office and eyed the baseball bat leaning on the wall by the door. A grin crossed his face at the thought that entered his mind. Sheriff Winslow glanced back as Wheeler grabbed the bat. Wheeler smirked. "Never know if it could come in handy."

CHAPTER THIRTY

Derrick crouched down and tried to lift Cassie to her feet.

"Stop, you can't. I'm handcuffed," Cassie said.

Derrick ran his hand over the pipe and traced it to the wall. "All right, turn your head. I'm going to try to break the pipe." He stood and kicked it several times without success. "Damn." He returned to the door and looked out.

Muffled voices drifted from the swamp toward them and Cassie's heart thudded in her chest. "Hurry, they're coming," she said.

"Damn," he repeated and tried to kick the pipe again. This time it loosened. He kneeled down in front of her and yanked the pipe from the wall, then slid the cuffs over the top. "Come on, get up," he said as he lifted her to her feet. He returned to the door and peered out. "Okay, hurry. Quiet! Go left and jump off the porch, then go around back."

As instructed, Cassie jumped from the porch and slithered along the side of the shack toward the back. Her body oozed with cold sweat. She bumped into someone and her eyes bulged. A small sound escaped her throat before Derrick grabbed her from behind and covered her mouth.

"Shh, it's Jess. Calm down. You clear?"

Cassie nodded behind his hand and he removed it. She shot forward and grabbed hold of Jess by the arm with her handcuffed hands. "Oh my God! I thought you were dead!"

"I would have been if it wasn't for the fog being crazy thick," she admitted through her tears. "They couldn't see through it. Then the weirdest thing happened—it cleared all of a sudden and Derrick was there."

Derrick moved past them and looked out into the swamps. "Come on. I have a canoe about a quarter mile back."

"Geesh, Derrick. Some getaway," Cassie quipped.

They trudged through the swamp, sometimes in waist-high water, sometimes on mucky ground, winding their way through the thick, mist-covered bayou. Ominous tree shadows made Cassie gasp more than once. "Anyone else feeling like Snow White right about now?" she whispered.

Jess let out a soft laugh. "Snow White?"

"Yeah, when she ran through the Forbidden Forest and all the trees grew eyes and claws and tried to grab her," Cassie said.

Jess shook her head. "You're so weird."

Cassie stopped and stretched out her arm. "Shh. Hear that?" She looked at Derrick. "Is it them?"

"Yeah. And they're getting closer. We have to hurry," he said.

A soft breeze stirred along the back of Cassie's neck and a whisper brushed her ear.

Go back.

"Guys, wait. I'm not sure we're going the right way. We need to go back, I think."

"Go back? Are you crazy?" Jess scoffed. "They're back there. I'm not going back. We need to keep going that way, toward Derrick's boat."

"She's right, Cass. We can't go back," Derrick said.

Cassie moved her cuffed hands to her throat. "I can't explain it, but I feel we need to go back. I feel like we're being warned. The mist...I mean, I just think—"

"Not happening. You've been telling those stupid stories about the swamp talking to you for so long, you're even beginning to believe it's true. We're not going back," Jess said and continued forward.

Cassie and Derrick looked at each other for a moment longer. "Fine," Cassie said and followed behind Jess.

They trudged through in single file. Jess held onto Derrick's shirt, and Cassie held Jess's arm. The land broke and they were in the water once again. Cassie squinted against the clouded night sky. "It's so dark. I can't see anything in here."

"Oh my God! Something just touched my leg," Jess whispered.

Derrick jumped. "Ugh! Mine too. Quick, over there. Get back on land."

Derrick and Jess climbed out first, and then helped Cassie. Even in the murky darkness, the look on Jess's face froze Cassie in place. "What?"

"Cassie, hurry! There's something coming at you."

They both grabbed her and pulled her from the water as the large snake slithered past.

"Hey, George, over there! I see them," Drakes called.

"George?" whispered Jess.

"Hank's brother. He wasn't here earlier. They must have called him."

"Run!" Derrick yelled.

"I got 'em," George said. "No worries."

A shot rang out and Derrick fell to the ground. Jess screamed and dropped down beside him, followed by Cassie.

"Derrick, talk to me," Jess said.

A second shot rang out and Hank's voice cut through the air, "*Noooo.*"

Derrick groaned in pain and held his hand to his shoulder. Cassie placed her cuffed hands over his and felt the fluid warm his shirt. "He's bleeding bad."

"What are we going to do?" Jess asked shakily.

"We have to stay calm. We have to keep our heads."

Jess crouched beside Derrick, shaking her head and rocking back and forth.

"Jess, do you hear me?" Cassie said. "We have to keep it together. Can you do that?"

Jess paused and then slowly nodded. "What now?" she quivered. "They're not far."

"I know. Derrick, can you walk?"

Derrick moaned but pulled himself into a sitting position with Cassie's help.

"Jess, you have to help me," Cassie urged. "Slide his arm over your shoulder to support him. I'll get the other side."

They tried to move quickly but Derrick kept sliding off Cassie.

"Dammit, Cass, you have to hold him."

"I'm trying! It's a little difficult to do with my hands cuffed, ya know?"

"You see them?" Drakes yelled.

No response.

Derrick stopped and knelt down. "That's close. We have to stop or they'll find us for sure."

Cassie and Jess knelt beside him. "Even if we make it to the boat, there's no way we're going to get down the river without them seeing us," Jess whispered.

Cassie looked around wildly for an escape. The sound of water and branches breaking behind her made her freeze. She crouched lower and pulled on Jess's arm. "Someone's coming."

"Look at that," Jess said and pointed at the mist.

The mist swirled around them and rose above their heads, hiding them.

A moment later Hank pushed through and nearly fell on top of them as he stumbled to the ground. Jess squealed and attempted to stand. Hank grabbed her arm and pulled her down.

Cassie lurched forward into Hank. "Let her go!"

Hank raised his arms to fend her off and pushed her down to the ground. "Stop!" Cassie and Jess continued to fight him. "Cassie, stop. I'm going to help you," he said in a firm whisper. He wrapped one arm around Jess and grabbed Cassie by the handcuffs to stop her movement.

"What do you mean?" Cassie asked.

Hank held his finger to his lips. "Listen."

"I don't hear anything," Jess said.

"That's good. He must've gone the other way," Hank said.

"Is your brother here?" asked Cassie.

Hank didn't answer.

"I heard the other guy call out his name," she said.

"Yeah, he's here," Hank mumbled. "Drakes shot him, and then turned the gun on me."

"Oh my God, Hank. Is George dead?"

"I don't know. I couldn't find him. Drakes has double-crossed us. I think he's working for Larson now." He sat back on his heels and rubbed his hands together in a nervous twitch. "I'm sorry, Cassie. I didn't want any part of any of this. I'm sorry about your daddy too."

Cassie's skin chilled. "What do you mean?"

"Drakes killed your daddy and old man Miller."

"I don't understand. What are you saying?" Cassie said. The words left her mouth without her mind's consent.

"Your daddy's death weren't no accident. You've been right all along. Larson hired Drakes to warn your daddy that if he knew what was good for him, he'd sell off his land. Georgie and Drakes was just supposed to scare him. Georgie wore a ski mask, hid in the boat, and waited for your daddy to come. When he did, Drakes jumped out at your daddy and grabbed him from behind. They had a big fight and Drakes knocked him in the head with his gun. Then your daddy hit his head on the boat and went under the water."

"This can't be happening. Why are you telling me this now?"

Hank shifted on his knees and peeked his head above the mist. "Cuz'in I might not be here come mornin'. And you and your momma deserve to know the truth."

"That you killed my father? Is this confession supposed to make me forgive you?"

"Not me. I wasn't even there. Georgie said he never thought your pa would put up a fight like he did. Before Georgie knew what was happening, your daddy was dead."

Cassie's mind darkened with fury and she leaped at his face with her fingernails. "You murdered him!" she yelled. "You bastard!"

Hank grabbed her wrists and pushed her back. "Cassie, stop. He'll hear you and then you'll all be dead."

Cassie froze.

Jess gasped. "Why do they want us dead? What did we do?"

"Nothing. Everythin's just got out of control. Georgie and Deputy Wheeler thought of a way to get money out of Mr. Larson. Him and Wheeler made a plan to kidnap Jess and order Larson to pay us fifty thousand dollars a piece in order for us to keep our mouths shut. Oh, and the fake Breathalyzer results too. Wheeler said with the campaign, Mr. Larson wanted to win so bad that he would pay anything to keep his name clean."

"So he had my Breathalyzer faked?" Derrick asked.

"I think so."

"Why would he even want that?" Derrick moaned.

"Because you hit his daughter with a car," Hank said, and Cassie half-expected him to follow up with "duh." "And it give him a good reason to go for the Rhyne property. He got big plans for all that land."

"Bad enough to frame someone for it?" Jess asked.

"Seems he already has 'vestors who gave him money upfront. He's in too deep. I thinks he's getting pretty desperate since your momma won't sell." Hank laid his hand on Cassie and Jess's arms. "Shh."

"Where the hell are ya, boy?" Drakes called.

Hank leaned in close and whispered. "Stay down. I'm gonna distract them. You get Derrick and go back to the boathouse. Drakes put your cell phones in the old ice chest. I'll try to lead 'em in the opposite way."

Cassie stared into his dark eyes. "Thank you."

Hank nodded. "I'm real sorry."

Cassie started to get to her feet then stopped. "Hank, did Noah know about my father? I mean, what really happened?"

"My paw? No. Georgie made me swear never to tell. He said he'd kill me if I did."

Cassie closed her eyes and sighed. She reached down and pulled Derrick to his feet and slipped under his arm. Jess repeated her move on his other side. Cassie looked at Hank and gave him a weak smile. "Be careful."

Hank nodded. "Now go." He ran toward Drakes's voice, making noise and breaking branches.

"I see ya, boy," Drakes called.

Cassie watched as he raised his gun and aimed it at Hank. A shot rang out and Hank moaned and fell.

"Gotcha." Drakes made his way further away from them as he went to check on Hank's body. "Dammit, where'd you go?" His voice carried through the night.

Cassie half stood and nudged Jess. "Come on." Derrick's head bobbed. "He's losing too much blood. We have to stop the bleeding,"

"We can't stop. They'll catch us," Jess said.

Derrick coughed. "She's right. Just get me back to the boathouse. We can call for help from there."

They continued on and were within fifty feet of the boathouse when Derrick stumbled to the ground.

Cassie dropped to her knees. "Dammit, I told you!"

"Come on, Cass, help me pull him. We're almost there," Jess said.

"No, he can't go any further. Go to the cabin. Hank said the phones are in the ice chest. Call your dad."

Jess ran off and Cassie tapped on Derrick's face. "Can you hear me? Stay with me. We're getting help."

Derrick's head rocked from side to side and he moaned incoherently.

"Come on, Derrick. Don't do this to me. You can do this."

Derrick coughed again and then he was still. Cassie stared down at him. She touched his throat. Her eyes closed and silent sobs racked her body.

CHAPTER THIRTY-ONE

Sheriff Winslow turned the car in the direction of Bayou Rhyne and the back of the Miller property. He pulled up at a stop at the intersection of Main and Mason and stared out into the beam of the approaching headlights across the street.

"Sheriff?" Wheeler asked.

A car pulled up behind them and waited. Winslow didn't move. The driver beeped.

"Sheriff, you're holding up traffic," Wheeler said and touched his arm.

Winslow regained himself, cleared his throat, looked both ways, and then turned left onto Mason. "Sorry about that. Lost in thought."

"Not a problem. I understand," Wheeler mumbled.

Winslow gazed out his side window. "You want to tell me what's up with you and Larson?"

"What do you mean?"

Winslow focused on the road. "I mean, you're at his beck and call.

The man shows up and you drop everything to take care of him. It's annoying, really. You work for me, not him."

Wheeler shrugged. "Think you're just paranoid."

"Does Larson have anything to do with the Anderson boy being missing?"

Wheeler stiffened. "Not as far as I know."

"All right, then maybe you can help me out with something else."

Wheeler glanced over at Winslow with a small smile. "Sure."

"The Breathalyzer," Winslow began. Again Wheeler stiffened. "I'm struggling a little with the .08 count. The kid seemed distraught, but not buzzed."

"Sir, I—"

The car radio crackled and then Mary's steady voice sounded. "Dispatch to car 62, shots fired at 3217 Rodney Lane. Can you respond?"

Winslow and Wheeler stared at each other, and then Wheeler pulled the microphone from the radio. He lowered it to his lap and looked at Winslow. "That's the Miller place."

Winslow switched on his lights, pulled a U-turn and headed toward Jefferson. "Yeah."

"Mary, we're already responding to shots fired. Is this a second report?" Wheeler asked.

There was a brief pause. "Yeah, it's a second call. I know how to do my job."

Winslow smiled. "Ask her who called it in."

"Who called it in?" Wheeler said into the mic.

"Noah Hickman."

Winslow's pants pocket began to vibrate. He pulled out his cell phone and glanced at the screen. "What the hell? Hello?"

"Dad!"

"Jess! Where are you? Are you okay?"

"No. You have to come quick. You have to help us. We're at the old Miller place at the boathouse. *Hurry.*"

"Whose there with you, honey?"

"Cassie and Derrick. Derrick's been shot and he's bleeding bad. Please, you have to hurry."

"We're on our way, honey. Who shot Derrick?"

"A man named Drakes. And Hank and George are out here too, but I think... I mean... I think they're dead, Daddy!"

"It's all right, sweetheart, try to stay calm. Where are they now?"

"Hank tried to help us get away. He made Drakes follow him away from us. But then there was a shot and... I'm pretty sure he's dead. I'm so scared. Please hurry."

"Okay, sweetheart. Where exactly are you now?"

"Behind the boathouse near the river. Derrick fell and couldn't get back up. Cassie is with him. I have to go back and help them."

"No, stay where you are. We're on our way. We'll be there soon."

Jess became silent.

"Honey, are you still there?"

Jess whispered into the phone with a shaky voice. "Daddy, someone's coming. I can hear them. Oh my God! They're going to find us."

"Jess? Jess!" Winslow yelled.

CHAPTER THIRTY-TWO

Cassie muffled her sobs at the sound of branches and leaves crackling. Her heart raced and her eyes bulged against their sockets as she strained to see. Branches cracked behind her and someone grabbed her arm. A small squeal left her throat.

"Cass, it's me. Shh. He's close," Jess said and pointed to her left.

They held their breath as the footsteps approached and slowly passed their position. The sounds eased off and became more distant.

"Oh, Jess, I think he's dead."

Jess knelt beside Derrick. "No. He can't be."

"I don't think he's breathing," Cassie said through tears.

Jess leaned forward and felt Derrick's neck. "How long has he been like this?"

"A few minutes."

"There's no pulse." Jess tipped Derrick's head back, pinched his nose, and breathed into his mouth. Then she started compressions to his chest. "I need you to help me. Watch me, and then do what I'm doing. Count, one, two, three, four, five, all the way to fifteen. I'll do the rescue breaths. Then we'll switch."

"I can't," Cassie said. "My hands are cuffed."

"Yes you can, and you will. That doesn't matter. Stop crying and get over here."

After the third set, fresh tears began to fall. "It's not working."

"Just keep going—"

Derrick coughed, rolled his head and began to vomit. Jess rolled him over to his side.

"Jess, you did it! You did it!" Cassie leaned over Derrick. "Derrick, can you hear me?"

"Yeah," he said in a weak voice. "Stop your fussing."

Jess leaned back on her heels. "Thank God for summer camp first aid class." She glanced around quickly. "We can't stay out here in the open. They're coming. I called my dad and he's on his way. He wants us to go back to the boathouse."

A soft, cool breeze floated under Cassie's hair and fluttered by her ear. *Boats*, it whispered. Cassie stretched up on her knees and peeked over the brush toward the river. "There, behind the boathouse. See those two overturned row boats? We can hide under them."

"You've got to be kidding. There's no telling what's under there."

"The mist—I mean, it's our best option," Cassie said.

Derrick moaned and coughed again. "I agree. We have to try."

"Can you get up?" Jess asked.

The girls pulled him into a sitting position and then helped him to his knees. "I'll try."

The three of them stood and scrambled through the swamp. Loud cries of crickets muffled the sounds of their movement. It seemed like eternity before they reached the boats. Cassie slipped out from under Derrick's arm and rushed forward. She kicked the side of the boat to scare any critters away, then lifted it, straining to see beneath. "I can't see, it's too dark. We'll just have to risk it." She returned to Derrick and Jess. "Come on, Jess. Help me get Derrick under the boat. I'll hide under this one with him. You get under the other one."

"I freaking hate this. I'm sure there's tons of spiders under there. And maybe even a snake or two," Jess said.

Cassie struggled to get down beside Derrick and Jess helped her pull the boat over them. "I'm sorry. We don't have a choice. Hurry."

"I know," Jess said and lowered the boat over them.

Cassie listened as Jess crawled under the other boat. Something small and light crawled on the back of her leg and she held her hand over her mouth so she wouldn't scream. When it was gone, she tried to forget it was under there with her. "Derrick? Can you hear me?"

Derrick didn't answer.

Cassie nudged him. "Derrick?"

"Yeah, sorry, I keep drifting in and out. My shoulder is killing me; the pain's so bad."

"Jess said her father's on his way. Just hold on. You have to make it through this."

"You care?"

"Of course I care. What a stupid thing to say."

"You love me?"

"Derrick, really…"

"Do you love me?"

"Yes," Cassie whispered.

"I love you, too. And I think I've proved that I would die for you."

"Yes, you have."

"Does this mean you forgive me?"

"I—"

Drakes's voice croaked from above the boat. Cassie's heart thudded in her ears. A moment later a pair of boots shown under the two inch gap between the boat and the ground. Slowly, the boat began to rise. A scream edged in her throat as she rolled to meet her pursuer. The sound of an engine drifted through the distance over the river. Drakes dropped the boat and the heavy thud of his boots rumbled on the ground as he ran away.

The boat passed by and Cassie listened to its fading sound, too scared to come out from beneath her hiding place. She listened carefully and hoped desperately that Jess had stayed put as well.

"Derrick," she said with a nudge. "Derrick, wake up. We have to go."

Derrick stirred and moaned.

Cassie slipped out from under the boat and crept over to the other one. "Jess? Can you hear me?"

Jess lifted the side of her cover and stuck her head out. "Yeah, what are you doing?"

"Drakes ran when he heard the boat. Did you hear it?"

"Who do you think it was?" Jess asked.

"I don't know. We have to hurry, we don't have much time. We need to flip this boat over and get Derrick down river to his truck. He said he parked about three quarters of a mile away. Then we can get him to the hospital."

Jess crawled out completely and crouched beside Cassie. "If we all get in that boat, we'll be sitting ducks on that river if Drakes comes back. Besides, my dad said he was on his way. I'll call him again."

Cassie frowned. "What's wrong?"

"The stupid thing isn't working. Let me get back in the boathouse. It worked in there last time."

"God, Jess, be careful," Cassie said.

Jess climbed the stairs and disappeared inside. A moment later, she jumped from the porch and headed back to the boats. "It's no use. I don't know why, but it isn't working now." Jess glanced up at the sky. "It must be cloud cover. We have to wait for my dad. He'll be here."

"That was probably him who passed us and Derrick is running out of time. Maybe your father got confused. Where did you tell him we were?"

Jess gave Cassie a sarcastic look. "At the boathouse. Where else would I have said?"

"Sorry." Cassie lifted the side of her boat and glanced under at Derrick. "Help me flip this over. Be careful not to drop it. We don't want to make a ton of noise."

They each got an end and began to turn it over.

"It's heavier than it looks," Jess said.

"Yeah, but don't drop it."

They lowered it to within a foot from the ground and Jess grimaced, "I can't hold it—" and the boat slipped from her grasp. A loud crack sounded as it landed on the corner of the other boat.

"Dammit, Jess, I said *not* to drop it."

"I couldn't help it."

Both girls looked around wide-eyed.

"Shh, get down." Cassie strained to listen for approaching footsteps, but heard nothing. "Come on, hurry up."

"I really think we should wait for my dad. If we leave here, he won't be able to find us."

"We can't wait. What if he doubles back?"

Jess grabbed Cassie's arm with a shaky hand.

"What is it?" Cassie asked.

"Listen. I think I hear something."

Cassie broke from Jess's grip. "Get Derrick's feet."

Jess stood frozen.

"Come on, Jess! Get his feet. Help me get him in the boat."

Jess grabbed his feet and together they slipped Derrick into the boat. "I'm pretty sure that if the gunshot doesn't kill him, we probably will by lugging him around like a sack of flour."

"What choice do we have?" Cassie knelt down and stared at his face, then looked hard at Jess. "Listen to me. Like you said, we can't all get in this boat and head down river."

"Yes we can."

"No, we can't." Cassie stared hard at Jess. "If we try to do this together, we could all end up dead. You take Derrick and go. I'll try to lead Drakes away from the river and deeper into the woods. Now go! Hurry. They're coming."

"Are you insane? We're not leaving you here." Jess grabbed Cassie by the arm and pushed her toward the boat. "Get in."

Cassie pulled away and stood up. "No. You get in, Jess. You're running out of time. Don't worry about me. I'll be fine. I have the mist to help me…to protect me. And it will protect you, too."

"Cass, don't be stupid."

Cassie backed away. "I'm not. Now go." Then she spun away and ran toward the front of the boathouse.

###

Jess stared after her, thoughts racing through her head. Everything in her told her to run after Cassie, but Derrick's condition was getting worse by the minute. He moaned and she glanced at him and then back to the empty place where Cassie stood only a moment earlier. Branches broke to the right of the boathouse.

"I see you, child," she heard Drakes call out. Then more branches broke and a gunshot echoed through the swamp, followed by a high pitched squeal.

Jess slapped her hand to her mouth to stifle her scream. Tears streamed as she looked down at Derrick. "What was she thinking?"

With a racing heart, she shoved the boat into the water, jumped in, grabbed the oar, and paddled quickly and quietly away as the mist silently rose above the river bed.

CHAPTER THIRTY-THREE

"Over there." Sheriff Winslow pointed ahead at the blue lights flashing from the patrol SUV on the side of the road. "Tomlinson's already here. He's putting the Marine 3 in the water." Winslow squinted past the SUV. "What's that? Isn't that the Anderson boy's truck?"

"Looks like it," said Deputy Wheeler.

Winslow pulled up behind the SUV, reached in the back seat of the cruiser, and grabbed two flashlights from the emergency bag. He handed one to Wheeler. "Keep your eyes sharp. There's three of our kids out here and its dark as hell. No mistakes."

Wheeler nodded.

They exited the cruiser and walked down to the water's edge. A light shined in Winslow's eyes. "Dammit, you trying to blind us?" Winslow said.

"Sorry, Sheriff," Tomlinson said. "We're ready to go."

Winslow and Wheeler trudged out to the boat. "Right," Winslow said. "Jess said there's three men out here. Two are the Hickman boys, but she thinks they've both been shot, maybe dead. Drakes is armed and dangerous. Wheeler already called for backup. Jacobs and Sanders should be here soon."

"Billy Drakes?" Tomlinson asked.

"Yeah," Winslow said.

Tomlinson breathed a slow and low whistle. "Not good. Not good at all."

Winslow glared at him. "Yeah, I know. They've already shot the Anderson boy."

"Dead?" asked Tomlinson.

"Not when I spoke to Jess." Winslow climbed into the 18 foot, flat bottom, single engine boat, laid his rifle on the floor, and started the engine. Wheeler and Tomlinson followed. "Let's move out."

They headed up stream about a half mile when Tomlinson tapped Winslow's arm. "Slow down, I see something ahead," Tomlinson said.

Winslow aimed the spotlight straight ahead and the shadow of a small rowboat appeared. He tapped the accelerator and pulled up beside it. Two bodies lay cuddled together.

"Oh, God," Tomlinson whispered.

Winslow shined the flashlight onto their bodies and the girl stared wide-eyed up at him. "Jessie! Thank God." He said and leaned over the boat and hugged her. "Are you hurt?"

"Daddy!" she cried. "No, but Derrick is. He's been shot. Please, you have to help him." Her voice shook with panic.

"All right, all right," Winslow said. He looked at the deputies. "Wheeler, call this in and get an ambulance en route. Tomlinson, help me get Derrick in this boat, then take them back to the road."

Tomlinson grabbed two blankets and carefully covered Derrick and Jess. "Good to go," he said.

Sheriff Winslow and Deputy Wheeler got into the smaller boat. Winslow faced Jess. "Where's Cassie?"

Jess's face contorted and she broke into sobs. "I'm so sorry. She ran off before I could stop her. She said she was going to distract them so I could get Derrick down river."

Winslow inhaled deeply and clenched his jaw. "Is she alive?"

Jess shook her head. "I honestly don't know. I heard a gunshot and then I thought I heard her cry out. I'm not sure." She bowed her head. "I'm so sorry I left her. I didn't know what to do."

Winslow squeezed his fists and looked at Wheeler. "It's okay, honey. You did the right thing. You had to get Derrick out of there. If they'd seen you…well, who knows what they would've done. Where was the last place you saw her?"

"At the boathouse. She ran into the woods toward the smoke house. Then…"

"It's all right. You did good. Tomlinson, get these kids to safety. The ambulance should be there a few minutes after you. Hurry." Winslow and Wheeler grabbed the oars and headed back upstream.

"Dad, no. Don't leave me!" Jess yelled after them.

Winslow glanced over his shoulder but continued on.

A few minutes later, Winslow drifted to the bank behind the boathouse. He signaled Wheeler to cut around the back and enter the woods on the east side.

They crept slowly through the woods, about twenty-five feet apart.

A cacophony of crickets screamed in the still, damp night. Cracking branches pulled Winslow to a stop, and he aimed his pistol in the direction of the sound. Wheeler stopped and aimed his rifle toward a different spot. Winslow glanced back and nodded for Wheeler to move forward.

Wheeler took several steps then stopped, his gun still aimed straight ahead, then yelled out, "Stop, lower your weapon."

Winslow scanned wildly ahead of Wheeler and saw the shadow of a man a split second before shots rang out from both directions. The shadow fell…and so did Wheeler.

"Wheeler, you hit? Wheeler!" Sheriff Winslow called as he scanned the area, making his way toward him. A noise in the brush to his right made him pull up. "Stop and raise your hands."

"I'm coming in. Now don't go shootin' me."

Sheriff Winslow's eyes narrowed at the sound of the voice. "Noah, is that you?"

"Yeah, boy." Noah reached Winslow and stood before him. "Found my boy George a few paces back. Okay I go check 'im?"

"Yeah, of course. I'll check on my deputy."

Winslow found Wheeler lying still behind a fallen tree trunk. He crouched beside him and felt for a pulse. None. He hung his head and sighed. He made his way to where the other body had fallen. Drakes laid panting in a marshy puddle. Winslow knelt down beside him and checked him out. "Where's the girl."

"Don't know. Couldn't find her in this pea soup of a fog. Dumb girl bested me."

Winslow assessed Drakes's injuries. "Looks like you'll live, but you ain't going anywhere. I'll be back for you." He crouched low and made his way to Noah.

"Noah, how's your son?"

"Dead." Noah grunted. "Those young'ns get away?"

"Jess and the Anderson boy are headed downstream to an ambulance now." Winslow squinted his eyes and glanced around. "The Rhyne girl is still out here somewhere."

Noah's faced dropped. "No," he breathed. "We best get findin' her. These swamps ain't no place for a kid to be alone."

Sheriff Winslow handed Noah the deputy's flashlight and aimed his own into the darkness. "This fog is so darn thick. I've never seen it this bad."

They walked about fifty yards when Noah pulled up short and shown his light slightly to his left. "D'you see that?"

Winslow looked sharp to where the light shown. "No, what'd you see?"

Noah paused. "I think I saw a woman."

"A woman? Out here at one o'clock in the morning?"

The mist swirled and a woman's shape rose above it. It shifted left and a path cleared through the fog. The men exchanged a glance and then moved slowly forward.

Again the fog thickened and the shape of a man formed to the right. His arm stretched before him and another path cleared. The men continued to follow.

Noah grabbed Winslow's arm and stopped him. "Shh, hear that?"

Winslow stared at Noah and listened.

A distant and muffled sound rose through the air. "Help me!"

The fog continued to clear small paths in the direction of the voice. The men rushed forward and the cries grew louder.

"Help me, please. Somebody help me!"

"Cassie! Keep calling, honey. We're comin' for ya!" Noah called out.

"I'm here! I've fallen."

The fog cleared one last time to expose the upper part of Cassie's body.

"Whoa," Noah called stretching his arm out to stop the sheriff. "Quicksand."

"Cassie, try to stay calm. Don't move around too much. We'll get you out." Winslow yanked a dead branch down from the nearest swamp red maple tree and extended it out to her. "Grab on, Cassie."

"I can't reach. My hands are cuffed. Hurry, I'm *sinking*."

Noah grabbed the sheriff's right arm to help him lean more forward. "Try now."

Cassie forced her arms up through the thickness and grabbed on to the dead piece of bark. "I got it."

A few moments later her body lay on hard ground.

The sheriff and Noah leaned over her with worried faces. "Are you hurt, child? Have you been shot? Anythin' broken?"

Cassie gave Noah a weak smile. "I'm fine, Noah. I haven't been shot."

Noah leaned back on his heels. "Thank the Lord for that."

She turned to the sheriff. "There's another man out here, Sheriff. He's after me. He shot Derrick, and…"

More branches broke to his left. He stopped and aimed his gun. A man stood and threw his hands in the air.

"No, wait. Don't shoot. I give. I give! I'm not armed."

"Identify yourself," Winslow ordered.

"Hank. Hank Hinkman."

"Don't move or you're a dead man, Hank. I swear I'll shoot you where you stand if you so much as twitch an eye."

"No, sir. I'm not movin'."

Noah walked forward and slapped Hank across the face. "You trackin' that kid like she's an animal? What's wrong with you, boy?"

"No Paw! You got it wrong. It was Billy Drakes. He been huntin' them kids. I been tryin' to save 'em. Really. I ain't even got a gun."

Cassie interjected. "He's telling the truth. He's done everything he could to help us."

Hank pressed his hand to his side and slipped down to the ground.

"What's wrong, boy?" Noah said and bent down to him.

"I been shot, Paw. And Drakes shot Georgie, only I can't find 'im nowhere."

"I found 'im, boy. It ain't good," Noah said in a low voice.

"No, Paw," Hank moaned. "Not Georgie."

Sheriff Winslow moved forward and helped Hank to his feet. "Come on, Noah, we've got to get them out of here."

Deputies Jacobs and Sanders barged through the brush a moment later, handguns and flashlights drawn.

"Heard a girl screaming," Jacobs said.

"Yeah, we got her. Wheeler's dead and so's George Hickman. Billy Drakes has been shot, but he's still alive. I want you two to take Cassie and Hank back to the cruiser and get them to the hospital."

"Call me an ambulance for Drakes. I'll be bringing the dead bodies with us, too." Almost as an afterthought, Winslow called over his shoulder, "Then call my ex-wife and get her to the hospital for my daughter. I'll meet them there when we're done here."

"Will do, Sheriff," Jacobs answered.

Winslow watched them leave and then looked at Noah. "Sorry about your boy."

"He's tough," Noah said. "He'll pull through."

Winslow nodded but spoke no further. Instead, he patted Noah on the arm as they both made their way back to Drakes.

Noah pushed on ahead of Winslow without looking back. "He's a decent boy, Sheriff. Just got caught up by his brother, is all. Georgie has a way of makin' that boy do things he ought'n not to."

Winslow stared at Noah's back and his heart ached for the man. "As far as I'm concerned, Hank is a hero. If it wasn't for him, those kids would most likely be dead. That's what I believe and that's what I'm gonna tell the judge."

Noah's voice cracked when he spoke. "Thank you, Sheriff."

CHAPTER THIRTY-FOUR

It was half past lunch when Jess and Cassie entered the hospital. They emerged on the third floor—Belle's floor—and walked slowly down the hall, glancing in each room they passed. Cassie carried a Dunkin Donuts bag concealing a chocolate eclair and Jess carried a tray with three coffees.

They turned the corner and both looked at the numbers on the wall of the fourth room on the left—room 303. Belle's room. Cassie paused in front of the partially closed door and was about to push it open when she heard Frank Larson's voice coming from within.

"Didn't work out quite like we'd planned, but don't you worry none. Things will still work to our advantage. You'll see."

She pulled Jess's arm, urging her further up the hall. "He's in there with Belle."

"Who?"

"Her father."

"Scumbag," Jess mumbled. "My father says as soon as Drakes

wakes up he'll have plenty to put Larson away for a long time."

"Did the doctors say he'll wake up for sure?"

"Not for sure, but they seem pretty hopeful."

They continued up the hall and around another corner to room 314. Cassie pushed the door gently open and both girls peered inside. Derrick sat upright in the bed, changing channels with a sour look on his face.

"Now that's the face of a happy-to-be-alive guy," Cassie joked.

"There's like ten thousand channels on this thing and nothing to watch," he said and then a broad smile lit his face. But you've just brightened my day."

Jess moved in behind Cassie. "Hey."

"Hey back at ya."

Cassie looked back and forth between them. "Really? After all we've been through together and you guys can only come up with a 'hey' to each other?" She rolled her eyes and dropped the Dunkin Donuts bag on the bed.

"What's this?"

"Open it," Cassie said grinning.

Derrick stuck his nose inside the bag and took a deep breath. "Oh no you didn't. Is this one of their famous éclairs? No, you didn't." He pulled it from the bag, took a large bite, and laid his head back against the pillow, chewing slowly behind a grin.

Jess cleared her throat and moved closer to the bed. "Yeah, well I, uh, I got you a coffee to go with it. Black, right?"

"Right-o," he said through a stuffed mouth. "Thanks." Derrick's eyebrows furrowed slightly and his expression stiffened. "Hey, Jess,

I've been meaning to thank you. You know, for saving my life and all."

Jess's face reddened. "Yeah, wasn't much."

Cassie again rolled her eyes. "Hey, I need to go down the hall for a minute. I'll be right back. Besides, you guys seem like you need to talk some things out."

Jess shot her a don't-you-dare glare. Cassie chuckled as she walked towards the door and called over her shoulder, "You'll be fine," and then closed the door behind her.

She glanced around the floor to make sure the coast was clear, and then headed to the elevator. It opened on the second floor and she stepped out into the hall. The layout was the same as the third floor so she knew where to find room 218.

She rounded the corner and her steps suddenly became heavy, making her feel as if she were back in quicksand. Her heart raced and her mouth dried. She came to the closed door of room 218 and stood before it. With a deep breath in and a slow breath out, she gently pushed the door open. Her eyes widened and she gasped.

A man stood before her with a needle in the IV. He spun around on her and grimaced. Before she could react further, he reached out and grabbed her, closing the door behind her. "You!" Frank Larson croaked. "This is all your fault. None of this would be necessary if your mother would have just sold the land like I told her to."

Cassie struggled to get free from him. She tried to scream but his hand gripped over her mouth.

"You know what? I'm kinda glad you walked in just when you did. Now I can take care of both of you and no one will be the wiser."

Cassie bit down on his finger and spun away from him, but instead of screaming she filled with hatred and words flew from her mouth. "You'll never get away with this. Everyone already knows what you've done. You're going to pay big time. I hope you rot in *hell*."

Frank chuckled with a sarcastic grin. "You fail to realize just who you're talkin' to, darlin'. You see, I'm going to be mayor of this town come two weeks from now and no one's gonna give a flying cow about this dirt-bag lying here. And you...well, you'll just be a poor, tragic accident."

"What do you mean? What are you going to do?"

Frank grabbed her once again and pulled her toward the door. The door burst open and hit him in the head knocking him backwards, dazed. Cassie pulled free and ran around the far side of the bed. Sheriff Winslow entered the room with his gun drawn. Frank regained his senses and rushed to the bed, holding the needle next to Cassie's neck.

"Don't come any closer, Sheriff."

"Easy, Frank. Don't make me shoot you. Put the needle down and step away from the girl."

"This isn't right. This wasn't supposed to be like this." He glared at Cassie. "This is all her fault. Her and that high and mighty witch of a mother."

"Frank, put the needle down and step away from the girl. Now."

Cassie elbowed Larson in the ribs at the same time her foot slammed down hard on his, and he weakened his grip enough for her to escape.

Frank slowly lowered the needle, his eyes wide and confused. "But this isn't supposed to be happening this way. I haven't done anything wrong. You can't prove I had anything to do with anything that's happened."

Winslow held his gun steady on Larson and nodded at the needle. "How about attempted murder right here and now?"

Frank looked down at the needle in his hand. "I found this here. I was going to bring it to you. Then the kid walked in and accused me of trying to cause Mr. Drakes harm. I was merely checking in on him."

"All right, Frank. Then just put the needle down so I can lower my gun, will ya? Then we can talk about it. When Drakes wakes up, I'm sure he'll clear all the muddy waters for us all. Cassie, I want you to come around the bed, slowly, and step out in the hall."

Larson put the needle down on the table by the bed and Cassie did as she was told. Once outside the room, Sheriff Winslow moved closer to Larson, turned him around, and handcuffed him.

"Wait! You said we'd talk about it," Larson yelled.

Sheriff Winslow clicked the handcuffs on and said, "Yeah, we'll talk down at the station house where I'll sit and listen to all you have to say. Right now, you're under arrest."

"You can't do this. Do you realize who I am? You can't do this!"

"Okay, Frank, calm down. Now, you have the right to remain silent and it might be a good idea if you did so right about now. Anything you say can and will be used against you in a court of law. You have the right to an attorney. If you cannot afford an attorney, one will be appointed for you. Do you understand these rights?" Winslow asked as he led Larson from the room.

Larson glared at Cassie while being escorted past her. "This is all your fault!"

Cassie smiled and winked at him. "Then I guess I've saved the town from the scum that you are. Take him away, Sheriff." She turned to a nurse and giggled. "I've always wanted to say that."

CHAPTER THIRTY-FIVE

Six weeks later

Hancock County Jail

The buzzer sounded and Belle walked through the heavy steel door into the long room with two rows of chairs separated by small glass cubbies with telephones. She walked past the first two cubbies and sat at the third. A guard standing on the other side of the glass nodded at her. A moment later the door opened and Frank Larson walked through.

The salty taste of tears stung the back of her throat. He stood and stared but didn't move. Belle stared hard in return. Frank moved forward, a small smile on his lips, and sat in the chair in front of her.

Belle slowly reached for the red phone on the wall, never taking her eyes from his. In turn, he reached for the phone on his side.

"Hello, sweetheart. I heard you woke up a couple of weeks ago. Are you feeling better? You know, getting back to normal?" Frank said.

Belle's throat swelled and she couldn't speak.

Frank's smile faded. "Did you just come here to stare at the freak show or do you have something to say?"

His snide attitude brought her back to her senses. "Now that I'm here, I don't really know what I want to say. I've thought it over a hundred times, but none of it seems right now."

"Belle, you know none of this is my fault, don't you? You know that whatever Drakes has said is nothing but a lie. My lawyers are working on it and they'll prove it. You'll see."

Belle squinted at him and tilted her head. "Really, Daddy? All lies?"

Frank nodded.

"What about everything I heard you and Deputy Wheeler talking about in my room? You know, when you thought I was nothing more than a…what did you call it? A vegetable?"

Frank's face stiffened and his stare turned to stone.

Belle smirked. "That's right, dear Daddy. I heard every word. Turns out people in a coma can hear and even see the people around them."

Frank glared at her through the glass with cold, hard eyes.

"What's the matter, Daddy? Trying to decide how best to silence me? Proving the word of an already known criminal false is one thing, but proving the word of your own daughter to be false is completely another. Do you want to kill me, too?"

Frank's eyes remained black and hollow for only a moment longer. A smile broke across his face. "Now, come on, Belle, don't talk like that. I'd never cause you harm and you know that."

"Do I, Daddy?" She slowly shook her head and grimaced. "How could you? How could you do such terrible things to all those people? Murder? I knew you were a lot of things, but I have to admit, even this was a surprise to me. And then to try to have my friends killed?"

"Your friends? Ha, that's a joke. You have no friends. You're just like me. You buy them."

"No, I'm not like you."

"Ah, little girl, more than you know."

"Then I'll dedicate my life to changing that. I want nothing to do with you, I want nothing from you, and I want never to be associated with you. I'm no longer your daughter."

"You'll always be my daughter, Belle." His eyes clouded over and his voice lowered. "You've hated the Rhyne girl since we moved here. You always wanted to bring her down. But I had the means to do it. I did most of it all for you. Don't you see that? Everything I did, I did for this family." His voice shook as he tried to contain himself.

"You must be joking. You self-centered piece of crap. None of this was for anyone but yourself."

"And what about you? What about all those nasty, mean, vindictive little things you did to those who crossed you or your path without permission? You see, my daughter, just like me."

Belle stood still holding the phone. "You're right. I did do a lot of terrible things to people, especially to Cassie. This family has caused the Rhynes far more pain than anyone should have ever had to go through. I have to try to set things right."

"Now hold on, Belle. Sit back down. When I get out of here, I'll help you. We'll work on setting this right together." He touched his palm to the glass. "I love you, Belinda."

Belle slowly returned the phone to its hanger and moved toward the door. When she looked back to her father, he still held the phone in his hand. She returned and picked up the phone. She wanted him to hear her words. She needed him to hear them. She didn't sit, only stood staring down at him through cold eyes. "I hate you and I hope you rot in hell for what you did." She replaced the phone and left the room.

CHAPTER THIRTY-SIX

Cassie sat on the white wooden fence of the round pen and watched the morning sun peek out from behind the horizon, painting the clear sky a deep shade of orange. She closed her eyes and leaned her head back, gripping the thin fence for support. A breeze tickled her neck and she smiled. Though no sound came from the wind, its tranquility caressed her skin.

"Whatcha doin?" a voice came from behind her.

Cassie's eyes shot open and she had to leap off the fence into the pen to stop from crashing to the ground. She spun around as Derrick approached with a grin.

"Ha, ha, very funny."

"I thought so."

"What are you doing here at this time of day? I thought mornings were your weak point," Cassie said trying to sound perturbed, but her smirk gave her true feelings away. She leaned her arms on the fence and squinted at him.

Derrick reached her and leaned over the fence to brush a quick kiss to her lips. "Nah, seems that getting shot has given me a whole new outlook on life. Mornings are now my strong suit, and so are afternoons and nights. I want to get the most out of each moment of the day, and I want to spend as many of those moments with you as I can."

"How do your parents feel about that?"

"Once the truth came out they've been nothing but apologetic," he said and leaned on the fence beside her. "You gonna come out of there so I can give you a proper hello?"

Cassie giggled and climbed through the fence. As promised, Derrick pulled her close in a bear hug and squeezed her tight. Strange how the feel of his arms gave her the same sense of security as the mist.

He lowered his lips to hers and kissed her long and deep. The familiar ache stirred low in her stomach and she moaned. He pulled back with a grin. "Glad I still have that effect on you." He reached into his pocket and pulled out a small crumpled tissue. "I was hoping you'd take this back."

Cassie's face lit like Christmas morning. "Hell yeah! I was afraid you wouldn't still want me to have it. I mean, I treated you awful."

"You kidding? After all I put you through, you still stood by me. No one else has ever believed in me like you." He tilted her chin. "I love you, Cass."

Cassie nodded with smiling eyes. "I love you, too. Come on, sit with me. I'm waiting for my mom to come out." She took his hand and pulled him to follow and Derrick gave a slight wince. "Oh, Derrick, I'm sorry. I should have realized."

"Not a problem. It's already been six weeks and I'm feeling great. It's healing really well, the doctor said."

"Yeah, but you probably shouldn't be driving or anything."

Derrick chuckled. "What am I supposed to do? Sit around my house for the next few months? Besides, I missed you too much."

Movement caught in Cassie's peripheral vision and she turned toward the upper barn with a smile and a wave to her mother.

Derrick followed her gaze and also waved. "So how are things between you and your mom?"

"Really good."

"I'm glad."

Cassie nodded toward her mother. "That's Cobalt Blue, the Henderson's new horse. Remember I told you about the new borders that came in last week? They call him Coby for short. Isn't he beautiful?"

"Wow, he's huge. What kind is he?"

"That, my man, is a Dutch Warmblood stallion. Incredible, right?" She cleared her throat and forced the threat of tears away. She glanced at Derrick to see if he noticed. He did.

"I know you miss him, Cass. I'm so sorry."

"Derrick, I thought you said you wouldn't keep doing that. You have to stop beating yourself up over it. It was an accident," she mumbled softly. "I understand what happened and I've forgiven you." She stared him in the eye and nodded once. "I've forgiven you."

"Have you forgiven Belle?"

Kate came within earshot and called out, "Derrick! Hi! Welcome back. We've missed you around here. How are you feeling?"

Derrick looked up over Cassie's head and smiled. "Hello, Mrs. Rhyne. It's good to see you."

"Still with that Mrs. Rhyne thing? How many times…never mind. I know, 'at least one more time, Mrs. Rhyne', am I right?"

Derrick blushed and Cassie smiled at his bashfulness and then poked him teasingly in the side.

"Knock it off," he mumbled with a grin and called out to Kate, "Yes, ma'am."

As Kate approached, Cassie opened the gate to the pen and stepped aside as her mother led in the large, beautiful beast. Again her throat tightened, but it was easier to push aside this time. Kate had told her that time would heal her wounds, but Cassie had to admit she never believed a word of it. Yet as time passed, little by little, as if against her will, Cassie found herself becoming less emotional. The feelings were still there, and the sadness, too, but the crying had nearly come to a complete stop. So did the anger. For the first time in what seemed like an eternity, the pieces of Cassie's heart began to mend.

"I'm on my way, ma'am," a voice called from the direction of the guest house.

The three turned to see Hank walking toward them, a slight limp to his stride.

"Just in time," Kate said. "Pick up that lunge line by the rock over there and bring it to me, will you?"

"Right, ma'am," Hank said.

Kate half-turned toward Cassie and Derrick and talked with tongue in cheek, "I don't know if I'm ever going to get used to all these ma'ams and Mrs. Rhynes, but I do kinda like it."

Cassie rolled her eyes and laughed. "Yes, ma'am."

Hank smiled and nodded at Cassie and Derrick as he entered the pen and closed the gate behind him. "I'm ready, ma'am."

"Good," Kate said and began the lesson.

Derrick and Cassie took up positions on the outside of the fence and watched as Kate showed Hank how to do ground work with the horse.

"You don't want to get on an animal this size without first lunging him. You want to work out any kinks he may have."

"Kinks?" asked Hank.

"Unruliness. They can be pretty full of themselves sometimes and you don't want to be on their back when they go into a happy frenzy, bucking and tossing their heads all over."

Cassie and Derrick silently watched for a while longer until she asked, "Think you can make it up to the weeping willow by the stream if we take the golf cart?"

"Sure, no problem."

"Good, let's go." Cassie waved to Kate and then they headed to the lower barn to get the cart. Cassie drove slowly up the dirt road of Weeping Willow Lane so Derrick wouldn't be bounced around.

"So, you didn't answer my question, Cass. Have you forgiven Belle?"

Cassie contemplated. "You know, I think I have. I haven't seen her since she woke up, but Jess has stopped by a few times and says she's doing well. Back to normal, really. And you know what? I'm glad for her."

"Normal? Is that a good thing?" Derrick joked.

She cast a sideways grin. "It's been hard, but yeah, I've forgiven her. I mean, look at the monster she has for a father. How could anyone be anything but cruel, self-centered, and egotistical living with that as an influence? Thank God she has Ruth Ann as a mother."

"Um, gee, tell us how you *really* feel."

Cassie chuckled. "I'm not trying to knock her. I'm just stating a fact. She is who she is. When I see her, I'm going to tell her I forgive her. She'll probably spit in my face, but I don't care. It's not my place to judge people."

"And things are good with you and Jess?"

Cassie pulled up under the weeping willow and parked. They walked to the stream and sat down at the edge. She picked up a small stone and tossed it in. "Yeah, looks like we're friends again. I like it." She chuckled. "I'm not so sure how Belle's going to handle it, though." She tossed another stone. "I should be asking you the same question."

Derrick picked up a piece of thick grass, placed it between his thumbs and forefingers and blew, making a loud honking sound.

"Cute," Cassie said.

Derrick smiled. "Yeah, we're good."

"Let's sit under the tree," Cassie suggested.

"Okay, but keep your eyes open. I don't want to lose a leg."

They lay in silent pleasure, intertwined together, kissing, touching, and loving. Cassie rested her head against Derrick's cheek and sighed.

"You okay?" he asked.

"I'm better than okay. I'm happy."

"I'm glad, Cass."

"Things are working out, aren't they?" she asked. "I mean, the world goes 'round no matter what. People—and animals—enter your life and then for whatever reason they leave, but they leave their footprint on your soul, never to be forgotten. I feel like time is healing my wounds, no matter how deep, just like my mother said." She gazed into the darkness of the marsh and smiled.

The sound of a distant horn broke the trance.

Derrick sat up. "What the hell?"

"I don't know. Come on."

Cassie drove the cart up in front of the lower barn and got out with apprehension. Kate stood outside the round pen talking with Ruth Ann Larson. "What do you suppose happened? I mean, why would she be here?" Cassie asked as she moved slowly toward Kate. "You think something's happened to Belle?"

"Not sure."

A movement caught her eye coming from the side of the trailer. A moment later, Jess walked around to the back and waved with a smile.

"Jess?" Cassie and Derrick exchanged a perplexed stare.

"Hi, Cass. Derrick," Jess called as they approached.

"Hey," they mumbled.

Banging from inside the trailer was followed by a well-known voice. "Are you going to help me here or what, Jess?"

Cassie's heart froze in her chest. She wasn't ready for this. Not now, not yet.

Jess opened the large steel door of the horse trailer and pulled out the platform. "Ready."

Cassie stared in at the backside of a very large and very white horse wearing four red leg wraps and a red sheet buckled in a crisscross under her belly.

"Okay, watch out. This girl's a big one."

The trailer thundered as the large animal backed out and then down the rubber padded platform followed by Belle leading her by a red halter and matching lead.

"Who's this?" asked Derrick.

The horse spooked slightly and stepped back with two quick steps. "Easy girl," Cassie said and reached for her shoulder. "She's beautiful, Belle. Andalusian, right? She'll be a nice companion for Goliath."

"That would be nice, but it's up to you."

"What do you mean?" Cassie asked.

Kate and Ruth Ann walked up and each stood beside their daughters. Kate placed a hand on Cassie's shoulder and smiled.

Belle stepped forward. A small smile touched her lips, but her eyes held a sadness Cassie had never seen in her before. "Cassie, I'm so sorry. Really, deeply sorry for the pain my family has caused yours and for the pain I've caused you. I don't ever expect you to forgive me, I mean ever, but I'd like to offer this three-year-old girl to you. Not that I think she could ever take the place of Arco, but maybe to ease the pain of his loss. That's why I got the complete opposite of him—white and female. I looked at many horses, and finally found her at a farm in Illinois. She came direct from Spain." She took another step closer and held the lead out to Cassie. "Please, Cassie."

Cassie stared in disbelief. Could she do this? Take another horse in place of Arco? But it wouldn't be in place of him really, would it? "She's so beautiful. I don't know what to say."

"Say yes," her mother nudged.

Cassie looked up at Kate through flooded tears. "But I don't know if I could ever love another horse the way I loved Arco. I'm not sure if I'd be good for her."

Belle let her tears fall as well. "Maybe not the same way you loved Arco, but in a different way, yet just as deeply and as special. I'm sure of it, Cass." She glanced at Jess. "It's what you're made of. I've always envied your gift for caring and for loving. I have no doubt that you will love her with your whole heart. There's room enough in there for both of them."

Cassie moved around the front of the horse and gently pulled her head down to meet her eyes. Her fingers rubbed small circles on her forehead. "Estrellita," she whispered. "Your name will be Estrellita."

A warm breeze drifted up her arms and the horse snickered softly.

"And I will love you, Essy, with all my heart."

###

LEAVE A REVIEW!

If you enjoyed the book, please remember to spread the word and leave a review at your favorite retailer.

ABOUT THE AUTHOR

Dee Ann Waite writes action adventure thrillers. Her first novel, The Consequential Element is a military action thriller (with a touch of romance) that takes the reader on a full throttle international ride from the streets of Boston to the jungles of the Congo.

Her intense interest in psychology, along with her studies in that area, have led her to her third novel, a psychological thriller titled Where Demons Hide, scheduled for release late 2015. This is the first installment of a three book series.

A former private investigator, and the sister of four retired brothers from both the military and department of corrections, as well as former FBI ties, the military and law have been a strong influence and have played out heavily in her writing.

Along with being an author, she has dedicated her blog to helping new authors achieve their dream of completing a novel and offers coaching assistance online, as well as with small groups throughout her community.

Dee Ann currently resides along the central east coast of Florida. When she's not writing, she enjoys spending time with her daughter and grandchildren, horseback riding, and nature. She owns a pet photography business and branches out her love for photography by visiting the Everglades and swamps in search of alligators and exotic birds. When at home, she cherishes a chilled glass of wine while sitting in her garden with her dog Dodger.

You can learn more about Dee Ann on her website at www.deeannwaite.com.

CONNECT WITH DEE ANN:

Twitter: @DeeAnnWaite1
Facebook: www.facebook.com/DeeAnnWaite
Goodreads: www.goodreads.com/DeeAnnWaite
Website: www.DeeAnnWaite.com
Send an email to: D.A.Waite1@gmail.com

This book is available in print at most online retailers.

MISTS OF BAYOU RHYNE

ACKNOWLEDGEMENTS

I don't believe any book is ever written solely by one self. It takes a village of people to complete a manuscript, and there are so many to whom I am grateful. For my sister, Carol Mahon, who first believed in my idea and then for helping me to shape it into what it has become.

For Michael Jarusiewicz, my best friend, and by all accounts, my better half, for his creation of the beautiful artwork for the cover of this book. Your unlimited patience and understanding, as well as your undivided attention through long fits of incoherent ramblings are priceless. Thank you for loving me.

For Rebecca Waite, my beautiful daughter, for encouraging me even when I wanted to give up. Your strength and fortitude give me the courage to continue onward.

And of course I'd like to thank my reading group, Liz Zook, Ivy Rasmussen, Anita Applegate, Diana Quiett, Melanie Linscott, and Erin Buteau. Thank you for your honest and valuable feedback. Without you this book would not be what it is today.

www.ingramcontent.com/pod-product-compliance
Lightning Source LLC
Chambersburg PA
CBHW071130200626
46817CB00018B/2524